PHANTOM SONG

(TOCCATA SYSTEM, BOOK TWO)

KATE SHEERAN SWED

Cover by miblart

Interior graphics by Chace Verity

✿ Created with Vellum

To Mom and Dad
I'm still working those music chops!

PART 1

OVERTURE

1

CLAIRE

Interplanetary Transport A90D

With all the various ways to die in space, Claire Leroux considered it a gross miscalculation that the only method of traveling through it was in a souped-up tin can that smelled like feet and French fries.

She'd never wanted to travel in a spaceship, ever. And yet here she was, standing at the window of a passenger transport, heart sizzling with anxiety as the ship navigated Landry's forest of satellites.

Claire liked to watch the satellites. From the ground. She did not like standing face to face with them, close enough to count their ugly tubes and solar panels. It was too easy to picture one—or all—of those complicated apparatuses breaking free to zoom through the vacuum and puncture her face. There was simply too much to live for, like music and kissing and Landry City's signature dark chocolate croissants, for her to be comfortable risking her butt up here. And all for the sake of Dad's company trip to Marya.

The crinkly standard-issue spacesuit she wore over her clothes felt like poor armor against the many, many dangers of space travel.

Claire hummed a tune under her breath to calm herself, an aria she'd been preparing for the upcoming round of summer theater auditions. *Sebben crudele, mi fai languir.* Her parents might force her into the black, and her girlfriend might encourage her to be more adventurous, but at least Claire could trust the opera—which was ancient, by the way, no change necessary—to provide an appropriately moody soundtrack. Cruel love. Languishing hearts. Betrayal, with a side order of doom.

The transport rockets fired gently, vibrating the floor, and Claire edged away from the glass. Surely people would start screaming if the movement were out of the ordinary. She darted a glance at the attendant who stood by the doors to the passenger lounge where everyone else was relaxing. He yawned.

Maybe she ought to call Iz, just in case. She didn't like the way they'd left things, that the last words she'd said to her girlfriend were that they were too different to make it work. Claire didn't believe that. She couldn't even picture a trip to the corner market without Iz.

If Iz were here, she'd point out all the good stuff. She'd describe the beautiful lakes on Marya and get Claire excited about toasting marshmallows or chasing birds, or whatever people did on other planets.

Claire had never left Landry before in her life.

The lounge doors opened, and Claire jumped. The attendant raised an eyebrow.

It was just Mom. She had her blonde hair tied back in a long ponytail, and Claire knew she was wearing blue jeans under her suit even though the rest of the passengers had dressed up for the trip. Claire regularly waffled between pride and embarrassed frustration at the level of her mother's confidence.

"There you are," Mom said. "Aren't the satellites gorgeous from up here?"

"I like them just fine from Landry City." Claire heard the sulk in her voice. She didn't care. Iz would tease Claire into cheerfulness. But Iz wasn't here, and Claire was stuck with her own grumpy devices.

Mom set a hand on her shoulder, the suit crackling as she moved. "We'll be back in two weeks. In the meantime, let's enjoy our adventure."

So far, adventure smelled like musty cheese and stale air. Also, there weren't any snacks. Not that her anxiety-squeezed stomach could take food at the moment, but it was the principle of the thing.

Claire was still trying to decide how to word her complaints when a loud blast echoed from inside the lounge. "Was that—?"

The attendant straightened and flew toward the lounge, then crumpled with a spray of blood as another figure flashed by the doors, too quick for Claire to see.

Gunshots.

The attendant's blood seeped into the grated metal floor. Claire wanted to help, or maybe just to look away, but all she could do was stand there in horror, staring at the perfectly round puncture in the man's forehead. Too late. Too late.

Mom shoved her against the window, cutting off her view. Even with one ear pressed against the plasticky fabric of her mother's suit, Claire could hear the startled passengers crying out from the lounge. She gagged, imagining she could smell the attendant's blood, though that might have been an illusion. The panic she'd contained since boarding the transport surged electric through her chest, and it took a concerted effort to clamp her mouth shut and stay silent.

Of all the disasters she'd expected today, a hijacking—or whatever this was—hadn't even entered her mind. Who would start a gunfight on a Landry transport? It was unheard of.

"This company left me with nothing," a voice boomed out of the lounge. Claire craned her neck despite Mom's hiss of protest, catching sight of a huge figure through the doorway. A bright green mask covered his face, the eyes flashing electric red. A shell of green-tinted armor protected the rest of his body, reaching up the neck and over the hands, revealing not a single sliver of flesh.

His feet were filed into blades.

Claire didn't recognize his voice, but Mom gasped as his raving speech continued and tugged her farther down the passenger bridge toward the emergency pod bay, still shuffling alongside the windows. Clearly this man was familiar to her.

Maybe it was the man's impossible size, or the mercenary shadows that flashed by behind him with weapons primed, but the sight of him sent a surge of primal terror rushing through Claire's veins. As if she were facing down a predator in the wild. When it came to fight or flight, Claire's body seemed determined to choose option three: freeze like a terrified rodent and avoid the eye of a hawk.

Mom, however, was in flight mode. She pulled Claire along the window toward the entry corridor. The man shouted something about debts, and then they were running.

"Who is that?" Claire asked. "What's happening?"

"He...I think he was injured in one of the factories last

year," Mom said. "They saved his life, but it was via... They used implants."

"Implants? Like they made him a cyborg?"

Cyborgs weren't treated very well in the Toccata System. Not that she'd heard of many incidents in Landry City, but there'd been that one incident on one of Marya's moons last year, where a cyborg entered a bank and the teller assumed she meant to hack into the system. Three security guards stunned the cyborg at the same time, frying her circuits. They hauled her off to jail before anyone realized she'd only been looking to make a deposit.

The bank wasn't even held responsible for the damage to the cyborg's systems. And when people talked about that day, their surprise centered around the fact that the cyborg had enough property to store in a bank at all. Jobs for cyborgs? They were nearly nonexistent. No wonder the bank officers had misinterpreted the situation, people said.

Dad thought it was wrong, that cyborgs were human beings with rights. Claire thought it was just the way things were. And yet Dad was the one trapped in the lounge with the mad cyborg, while Claire ran away. All because she'd needed a few minutes to sulk.

Mom pulled her along faster. "We need to get to an emergency pod, now."

"What about Dad?"

The lights went out, and Claire stumbled. Reflections from the satellites outside illuminated Mom's back in uneven strobes as they ran through the hall.

Claire asked about Dad again. Mom didn't answer. Claire had dragged her feet down this corridor less than an hour ago, surrounded by rolling suitcases and voices chattering excitedly over the rustling of spacesuits and automated safety announcements. The crowd had moved slowly, and in her mind, Claire compared them to cattle.

Now the corridor was empty. No matter how fast she sprinted, her churning adrenaline made it feel like she was moving through a vat of honey.

Seconds blurred, and they burst through a set of double doors, nearly colliding with a pair of men in full fatigues. Claire would have thought they worked for the transport company, except for the guns holstered at their hips. They shouted in surprise. Mom didn't pause.

Ahead, the emergency pod arches glimmered.

Mom caught her wrist and pulled her forward. Claire stumbled again and nearly fell, catching herself on the floor with one hand. Something in her wrist sent a painful jolt up to her shoulder, but she scrambled to her feet and kept moving. The pods seemed impossibly far away. Footsteps hammered behind them, and Claire shut her eyes, her uninjured hand stretching for safety.

She inhaled metal, and sweat. The footsteps pounded closer.

Her fingers brushed the frame of the first pod, and she opened her eyes.

Someone grabbed Claire's hair from behind, pulling her back so hard that she lost her footing. She tried to brace herself with the injured hand and cried out as pain radiated through her wrist. *Broken*, a still-functioning part of her brain whispered.

A scream ripped through the bay, and Claire twisted her head despite the hand in her hair. Her mother ran toward them, roaring like she meant to take the place down with her voice alone, a trio of men at her heels.

"No," Claire choked, but it was too late.

Mom slammed into Claire's captor, knocking him to the

ground and forcing him to let go of Claire. Her head slammed against the floor, but she righted herself, ready to rush to Mom's rescue. Before she could blink, Mom had the soldier's gun in her hand. She fired.

Still gripping the gun, Mom scooped Claire up and shoved her into the E-pod. Despite the pain that radiated up her arm, Claire tried to hold onto her mother's hand, but Mom wouldn't let her. Instead, she secured the straps over Claire's body and shoved an O2 helmet on her head, twisting to attach it to the suit.

And then she pulled away.

"What are you doing?" Claire said as the suit built gloves around her hands, an automatic reaction to the addition of the helmet.

Mom blew her a kiss and shut the pod door. She hit the button to pressurize.

"What are you doing?" Claire cried, but her mother couldn't hear. She faced the soldiers, gun outstretched.

She was giving Claire a chance to get away.

To hell with that.

Claire reached to unbuckle the safety strap.

The pod pressurized with a beep, giving her only a second's warning before it detached from the transport and shot away.

Claire screamed at her mother's silhouette through the firing of rockets. She saw Mom drop the gun, the men leading her away. Hand shaking violently, Claire placed that call to Iz. Some rational corner of her mind told her to phone the atmo guard, the police, *someone* in authority. But it was too late. There was nothing they could do.

Claire needed Iz.

The connection failed. Claire tried again, her breath heavy in her ears, eyes burning as she kept her attention locked on the transport. There was a cylindrical ship attached to the main airlock, and as she watched, it peeled away from the bigger ship, wheeling around to drop toward Landry like a tumbling meteor.

Claire surveyed the E-pod's controls. The mercs—or revenge seekers, or whoever they were—had gone. If she could figure out how to work the controls, she could get back to the transport. Find Dad. Hug Mom, and yell at her for not taking the pod's empty seat.

Flying was Iz's territory, but this was a standard E-pod. How hard could it be? Throwing a blanket of false confidence over her panic, Claire forced herself to look carefully, to think. In a few minutes, she'd be back onboard. No problem.

The lumbering transport exploded, snakes of fire curling inward toward the only available oxygen, and snuffing out as that gas leaked into the blackness.

Claire stopped breathing, hands still poised over the controls.

The tab connection clicked. Iz said, "Hello?"

She sounded worlds away.

A rainstorm of shrapnel fired out of the transport's center, a thousand bullets spinning toward her through the blackness.

Sebben crudele, mi fai languir.

Claire cut the connection to Iz and let them come.

2

CLAIRE

Trigin-North Medical Center
Marya Moon Triginti

W hen Claire regained consciousness, it felt like her body was encased in flame. She lay flat on her back, a light above her shining so brightly that her right eye squinted, streaming tears of protest.

When she tried to blink, her right eye closed. Her left didn't.

She tried again. Nothing.

Her left arm wouldn't move, either.

Claire swallowed a bitter wad of panic and forced herself to breathe. Her lungs worked. That was something.

Still staring at the offensively bright light, she twitched her right foot, and then her left. Knees, check. Thighs, good. Hips, all set.

Torso.

Chaos.

The left side of her upper body refused to move. Heart

skittering, Claire tried twitching her elbow, her shoulder, her fingers. She squeezed her stomach muscles and tried to roll, but it was as though she'd been pinned down. For a hysterical moment, she pictured butterflies trapped in shadow boxes, their wings spread in a permanent death display.

Disoriented, she tilted her head, trying to get a look at the room. Even that movement felt strangely heavy, the left side of her face dragging her back toward the sheet.

She'd been in an emergency pod.

There'd been a fire.

Her mother...

Claire swallowed again. She breathed. She wasn't in a pod now; she was lying flat, with a firm mattress behind her back. She opened her mouth to call for help.

Before she could make a sound, something soft landed on her stomach. A bag.

"Your medications," someone said. "You'll be immuno-suppressed for a month, so don't go licking any sidewalks."

Claire blinked—her right eye, anyway—and a nurse came into focus. She wore blue scrubs, a cap perched on top of graying curls, and a paper mask hooked over the bottom half of her face.

"I don't understand," Claire said, her voice rough. "Where's my mother?"

Fire and gunshots crackled in the back of her mind, whispering the answer. She shoved them away.

"Apparently she wanted this for you," the nurse said, a scowl fixed across the half of her face Claire could see. Claire imagined the woman's lip curling in disgust.

This.

Claire tilted her chin again to look down at her body.

Metal and wires. Bolts and gears

Cyborg.

No. No, that couldn't be right. Claire's family was dead. They couldn't have given the instructions to turn her into... They couldn't have. *Because they're dead*, her brain buzzed, repeating the refrain as a frantic mantra. Shouldn't she be upset? Crying? She couldn't feel. She didn't feel anything.

Shock, a calmer voice interceded. *You're in shock.*

The second voice sounded like Iz. Claire forced herself to draw breath.

The nurse stood over her, staring. Waiting for a response. When Claire said nothing, the nurse rolled her eyes. "You're fixed," she said, enunciating slowly. "You have thirty minutes to clear the premises."

Claire swallowed. Her throat felt like glue, but she didn't dare ask this woman for water. "I can't move."

"That is your affair." The nurse swept out of the room, and the door slid shut behind her with a clatter.

Hateful as she was, Claire wished the nurse would have stayed. There was no one else.

And no wonder. A cyborg. Claire was a cyborg now, like the man who'd destroyed the transport.

With that thought, memories crashed through the dam of her shock, vibrating her eardrums with phantom gunshots and screams, the pressure in her chest squeezing painfully as she watched her mother being marched away.

Again, Claire shoved the memories aside to focus on her body. Would she ever feel the metal side, or would it remain numb? She didn't know. But the nurse had made it clear: if Claire couldn't walk out of here, the hospital would show no mercy.

Claire allowed herself a single, shuddering breath. When she released it, a tear leaked out of her right eye.

With her right hand, Claire touched her face. On one

side, she brushed warm skin. Her chin. Her eyelashes. She ran a finger along her cheek toward her nose.

It was gone.

Or, more accurately, it had been replaced. This nose was made of solid metal, melded seamlessly to the skin, the bone and cartilage shaved away. Her nose, her left cheekbone, the left side of her jaw. All metal. Even the eye she hadn't been able to blink when she first woke up was robotic.

They might hate cyborgs in this hospital, but someone certainly knew how to make them.

Who would have ordered it? Who would have *paid*?

"How am I supposed to drive this thing?" she muttered.

It was a rhetorical question, but a stream of letters fluttered across her vision in response, obscuring her view and inducing a wave of vertigo. She squeezed her right eye shut and caught the tail end of the instructions: *...ready to begin, you may request initiation sequence in order to prompt robotic limb assistance. Refer to Appendix C to review potential risks associated with extended submersion and extreme electrical shock...*

Right. Operational instructions. Claire licked her lips and tasted metal. What else could this thing do? The letters marched on, directions crawling across the ceiling like a parade of ants. She wondered if it could present the information in audio.

Could she still sing? The thought seemed at once crucial and laughably frivolous. Who cared if she could sing? What could that possibly matter?

Claire cleared her throat. "Um. Start instructions over? Please? And can you read them to me?"

The body obliged, buzzing a step-by-step tutorial into

her ear. Under its guidance, she lifted her mechanical hand, twitched the fingers, and adjusted her shoulder position to avoid strain. She couldn't feel the metal side at all, but the more she moved, the more it felt like playing a musical instrument. Singing might be her dream, but she was passable at flute and guitar, too—enough to know how to treat an instrument as an extension of the body.

When she thought about it that way, the situation felt a fraction less dire.

Following the instructions, Claire got out of bed, shouldered the duffel bag without glancing at its contents, and left the hospital.

Once outside, though, she stopped at the curb. She had a right to stand on the sidewalk, surely, but no power over the glares of the people passing by—every one of whom gave her a wide berth as they passed. She thought of the woman who'd been stunned and arrested trying to make a bank deposit. *It's just the way things are*, Claire had told her father when he lamented about anti-cyborg sentiment. Privately, she'd even thought it made a certain amount of sense. Who knew what cyborgs could do? Hack systems? Punch through walls, or see through them? It was wise to be wary.

It's just the way things are.

Dad had argued in favor of compassion, always. Had he been passing by here, he'd have stopped to ask if she needed help. It took a concerted effort not to imagine it, her father appearing suddenly among the crowd of glares, smiling, with Mom hurrying along beside him.

But Claire couldn't think about Dad and Mom right now. She couldn't risk falling apart.

Maybe it would be better if she started walking. Maybe

this moon—one of Marya's, judging by the bloated, rust-colored planet hanging in the sky—had a busy port where she could blend in while she figured out what to do next.

As though in answer to her thoughts—or perhaps literally in answer to them; she'd need to research that—the cyborg-body voice piped into her ear. *Wait for Viv.*

"Who's Viv?" Claire asked.

"I'm Viv," a woman said, materializing at her side. She had dark skin and wore a flat-billed cap with a plaid design, gold studs shining in her ears. "Don't panic. You're safe."

That hardly seemed likely. Aside from Marya's presence in the sky, Claire didn't recognize this moon, its flat landscape and gray squat buildings. Landry City had a hover-rail; here, a steady stream of bicycles zipped through their own lane, while an oblong streetcar rumbled along golden tracks, its passengers pointing at Claire from the windows.

Manners were apparently optional here. But the streetcar passengers weren't the only ones to notice her. A doctor in a white coat crossed the street to avoid passing close, her rainbow ponytail swinging behind her as she hurried. A *doctor*. Even a patient with his arm in a sling stepped off the curb, forcing a bicyclist to swerve out of his way.

Claire stopped walking. "Who are you? Don't say Viv."

The woman gave her a kind smile. She was older than Claire, maybe in her twenties. Was Claire supposed to recognize her? "My employer finds girls like you, who are in trouble, and she rescues them," Viv said. "If you'll allow me, I'd like to take you to her. She has a job for you."

Claire stared, flabbergasted, waiting for Viv to laugh and tell her it was all some kind of a joke. Even better, to smack her and wake her up from a particularly vivid nightmare.

She'd find her parents waiting, and Iz. No cybernetic parts. No cryptic benefactors.

When neither happened, Claire said, "Who is she?"

"Her name is SATIS," Viv said. "But she'd like you to call her Mother."

3

ISABELLE

Five years later
Landry City Opera House

To Iz Chagny, the Landry City Opera house was both beautiful and terrible. The bowl-shaped auditorium was a legend of crystalline perfection, its lines shaped more like water than stone. The chandelier suspended in the center of the hall glittered with a thousand glass tubes, the showpiece of the already ostentatious theater. Staff patrolled the aisles in bustled skirts and top hats, ushering people to their seats with the help of cyber-glasses designed to look like monocles and holo-tabs that unfolded like fans. The smell of flowers permeated the theater, fresh blooms mixing with dried potpourri.

The opera house itself was beautiful. It was the memories that plagued Iz. She sat wedged between her friends, Jane and Mari, in the opera box they'd purchased for the night through the Star Leaders Academy. Her friends were more interested in scanning the crowds for celebrities than they were in the performance, which was set to begin any moment. Iz had heard rumors of the new director's edgy staging, with audience seats that moved to allow mini stages to rise in the center of the room—half opera, half ride—and actors making entrances via hovercraft. There was even talk that this year's Gala Night would include interactive VR experiences for the audience.

Box Five was so well placed that Iz and her friends would have no need for their gem-crusted opera glasses, yet Jane and Mari had produced nearly identical pairs and were using them to look back and forth across the lines of VIP boxes.

Searching crowds was supposed to be Iz's area of expertise. But every time she tried, her vision inexplicably blurred with tears. How many times had she been in this room with Claire clutching her hand?

She'd thought she was ready to face Landry City again. She might have been wrong.

"I hear this place is haunted," Jane said, nudging Iz's elbow and offering her the glasses. "Perhaps you'll see a ghost with those."

Iz sighed. "That's what I keep hoping."

Jane patted her hand. She knew that Iz had spent the past five years searching every crowd, every street, and every corner of the network for a sign of her childhood sweetheart. Everyone else believed Claire was dead, but Iz could never forget the staticky call she'd received *after* Transport A90D went up in flames, the sound of panicked breathing.

"I don't see Conor," Mari said.

"Probably stayed on *Traveler* to make love to that AI jammer of his." Henry spoke from behind them, a bitter edge touching his tone. Iz twisted to catch his eye, but her pilot colleague was in the same position he'd been since he tossed himself into the chair twenty minutes ago, leaning with his head propped on his hand and staring glumly at the floor.

Since Astra was nowhere in sight, Iz assumed they'd had a fight. She didn't particularly regret the sharp-tongued woman's absence, but she felt sorry for Henry.

"Why are you looking for Conor?" Jane asked, the glasses still glued to her face. "Got a crush?"

Iz expected Mari to deny it, but she just shrugged. Conor Keyes was as arrogant as he was handsome. Mari could do better. So could Henry, for that matter. Iz started to say that, but the chandelier dimmed, indicating the start of the performance.

Mari sighed and dropped the glasses to her lap. "Time for culture, I suppose."

"But we finally get to see this famous new soprano," Jane said. "Angelique D'Aae. Everyone's obsessed with her."

Mari just grumbled in response.

The orchestra struck their tuning notes as the auditorium came to life in mother-of-pearl iridescence. Whatever this new opera director had been doing, Iz was glad he'd preserved the nostalgia of the lighting scheme. The whole room sparkled.

The center of the stage twisted open, and a platform rose. The figure it carried was swathed in layers upon layers of costuming, blues intersecting with violets and greens and golds, with shadows playing around her gloved hands. A black veil hid most of her face, and there was a rose fixed behind her ear.

Even Mari sat up a bit straighter.

And then Angelique began to sing. Her notes rang through the theater, crystal as the chandelier, as she skipped effortlessly through her opening aria. A soprano, yes, but what a range; her low notes resonated with the beauty of ocean waves, her high notes ringing out like bells.

Her technical skill was inescapable, there was no denying that. But it was the emotion behind the melody that held the audience in rapt attention, the way Angelique lengthened an anguished note until she ought to have run short of breath, the way she guided the tempo as though the tune belonged to her alone.

Iz had only ever heard one person sing like that. Her throat went dry, and she nearly rose out of her chair, stopping herself just in time. Her hand went to her mouth, thoughts jumbling, and the room seemed to tilt.

It couldn't be her.

It couldn't be, but it was.

Layers of cloth and veils would never hide the truth. Not from Iz.

The famous opera ingenue was her long-lost sweetheart. It was Claire.

THE OPERA WAS TOO SHORT, and too long.

Iz could have listened to Claire's singing all night—that had always been true. While Jane and Mari chatted through the intermissions, Iz sat with fists clenched around the armrests, thoughts racing. Claire was here, at the opera. Had been here all along, maybe. Iz had searched for her in performance halls, of course, and combed the papers for mention of her name in connection with theaters across the system.

She had not thought of stage names or aliases.

Angelique. Of *course* it was Claire. Her music had commanded Iz's attention since they were children. She had known, hadn't she, that Claire would sing on this stage one day?

In the middle of the final act, Iz could take it no longer. She slipped out of her seat and bounded down the carpeted stairs of their box. She asked a startled usher how to get backstage, answering his surprised stammering with her father's name so that the poor man almost fell over himself to give her directions.

Three more times, she invoked it—Chagny, Chagny, Chagny—as she descended through levels of the opera house. Three more times, doors opened.

Iz didn't use Dad's name often, but there were times when it paid to be a famous hero's daughter.

Of course, it also meant she'd be hearing from the opera's development office. She'd donate anything they wanted, join their list of patrons in an instant if it meant seeing Claire again.

Iz stepped backstage to the rustle of costumes as the chorus prepped for the finale, and followed the last usher's directions around a corner toward the ingenue's dressing room. The walls closed around her, dark and narrow, and she stepped carefully to keep from tripping.

Her hands shook, and no amount of swallowing could moisten her throat. Belatedly, she remembered her pilot training had provided adequate resources for controlling her physical responses, but all she could do was to clasp her hands before her. At least there was no one lingering in this part of the corridor to witness her nerves.

The metallic shine of Claire's name—well, Angelique's name—gleamed on the door ahead, ornate flowers reflecting the glow of the lanterns in the hall. They seemed dimmer with each step she took, the floor growing more shadowed beneath her feet. Why would they tuck their star all the way back here?

Music still floated above her head, but the soprano's death notes had been struck while the tenor—and the audience—wept with sorrow. Iz knew this opera, knew the hero had a death-avenging recitative, and maybe an aria, left to sing before the curtain fell. Which meant Claire would be here.

Iz reached the door and raised a hand to knock. A strain of melody sounded from inside, almost too distant to hear.

For a moment, the sign reflected a pair of fiery eyes.

Iz whirled around, looking for the source. A figure whipped away into the darkness, the silhouette muddied by flowing fabric. Iz tripped after it, trying to ignore the way it seemed to float.

"Wait," she called.

Go, it replied—or something did—and a hot wind rushed along the corridor, supernaturally strong, urging Iz back toward the wings of the stage. Iz pushed forward, even as doubt wove through her confusion. Claire wasn't hurt. She wasn't lost. She'd survived the A90D disaster, and she hadn't bothered to come looking for Iz. They'd been in love, or so she thought. Why should she fight this...whatever this was, for the sake of someone who'd abandoned her? Why should she be here at all?

The lanterns went black.

Iz let the wind shove her back to the wings, where it died as the chorus rustled around her, rushing toward their final bows. The opera had ended sooner than she'd expected, which meant Claire might appear at any moment to accept the adoration of the audience.

Iz scrambled out into the auditorium, tears streaming down her cheeks.

Where she ran straight into Jane, who was arguing with the usher who'd allowed Iz backstage.

"They said you came this way, but apparently your hero father is a better ticket than my...Iz, are you all right?" Jane looped an arm around Iz's waist. "You look like you just saw a—"

"Don't say it," Iz interrupted. Back in the light of the theater, her doubts felt flimsy. "I need to go back there. Something was...but it couldn't have been..." Her thoughts crowded in, too many to organize. She tried to breathe. "I just need a moment."

"Can't, doll," Jane said. "That's why I came to find you. It's time to go. The Star Leaders transport waits for no stragglers. Which is a lie. They wait for everyone. Can you imagine the phone calls if they left us here? But everyone's supposed to come now."

Iz cast another look back at the door as Jane guided her to the exit, half expecting to see those fiery eyes staring back at her. But it was just a door, smooth as the rest of the auditorium's walls.

PART 2

RECITATIVE

4

ISABELLE

7 Days After the Opera
Verity's Upper Atmosphere

Iz's hands were slick on the controls, adrenaline surging through her body as she monitored the spaceship's ascent. She'd rocketed off planets more times than she could count, but she'd never done it under pursuit. Her breath still came hard and fast after sprinting half a mile across Verity's countryside to reach the ship. They'd barely made it.

Everything had gone wrong after the opera.

Conor Keyes had died. Iz had flown Astra Havis to her space station, where the would-be assassin's AI mother figure destroyed itself—and its evil plans for controlling the system—in a ball of fiery redemption. Somewhere along the way, Henry had turned up, too, though Iz still wasn't too solid on those details. And right now was a terrible time to clarify.

"At least three shooters behind us," Henry called out as the force of Verity's atmosphere tried to pull the pod back to the planet. The poor little ship was doing its best, but their pursuers had it out-engined by a long shot. They flanked the escape pod, guns drawn, as if they were simply headed out for an escorted stroll.

"Not much I can do til Iz gets us past atmo," Astra said, sounding unfairly calm about the whole thing. Her AI mother might have trained her to be icy in a crisis, but Iz didn't have a lot of experience with adventures of this magnitude. It seemed to her that system-saving heroics should be rewarded with rest interludes. Space for planning next steps. Things like that.

No such luck in this case, obviously.

Iz punched the rocket booster again, trying to urge the little ship into action. Not that it would do much good; the rockets were already pushing full capacity. "What can you do when we do break atmo?" she asked. It wasn't like her to let irritation leak into her tone, but she didn't have much patience for keeping it in check at the moment. This was all because of Astra, really. Not that Iz blamed her for refusing to join up with Edward Keyes and his band of thugs when he radioed that recruitment call, but still.

"I can shoot." Iz didn't turn to look at her expression—a lifetime of space racing told her to keep her eyes on the screens, even if she'd never raced under pursuit like this— but she could imagine Astra grinning. Wolflike.

She and Astra had a few philosophical differences when it came to problem solving.

"Hitting the rings in sixty seconds," Henry said. "Are you good, Iz?"

She and Henry were both in training—if the Star Leaders Academy still existed to train them after the explosive news stories about its AI being compromised, thank you Astra—but Iz could fly a mean space race.

Space *battles*, she wasn't so sure about. Reaching a goal ahead of her competition was one thing. Evading gunners? Not her area of expertise.

The rockets quieted, replaced by the comforting hum of the in-space engines. Astra was already out of her takeoff position, diving for the weapons control seat and the ship's unwieldy mounted cannon. A pod like this was not built for fighting; SATIS had obviously made changes.

Which, on a cozy ship like this, might explain the engine strain. Iz patted the dash sympathetically. The poor girl hadn't asked for modifications.

Astra's chair bumped into Iz's as she moved into position and locked her hands around the gun controls.

"Maybe we should avoid shooting," Iz said.

"Doubt they're going to be as charitable," Astra replied.

As if in answer, the ship hugging their starboard side swiveled its guns. The enemy vessels were sleek black, with orange tips. Like some kind of exotic bird.

Iz wasn't qualified to battle gunners, but what if she treated this like a race, instead of a shootout? Shift and dodge. Evade and escape. Cross the finish line ahead of the bad guys. Biting her lip, she pointed the pod's nose toward Verity's rings. From the surface, the rings looked like wide bands of moonlight that had been smeared across the sky.

From here, they looked like a rocky obstacle course.

"Hitting the rings in ten seconds," Henry said, eyes on the navigation panel. "Iz, we're headed directly in. That your plan?"

At this point, Iz didn't see another option. The other two ships were still hugging the pod's flanks. Surely they'd break away before hitting the rings. They'd have to.

"They won't follow," she said, trying to sound more confident than she felt.

Astra hissed out a breath. "Just get ahead of them so I can shoot."

Iz gritted her teeth. If she could pilot efficiently through the rings, they might avoid a firefight altogether. She pushed the pod into a last burst of acceleration, and the shield alarm flashed to life as pebble-sized rocks pummeled the pod's forcefield.

"You're supposed to avoid debris," Astra said.

"The rings are made of it." Concentrating, Iz clenched her jaw so tight her teeth squeaked. "I can only avoid the big stuff."

"The little stuff is just as bad at these levels," Henry said.

Iz swerved to avoid a spinning boulder, swinging the pod onto its side. "Not as long as our shields hold out."

The green bar on the dashboard faded to a sickly pea soup color before dropping quickly through yellow and on to dull orange. That was...much faster than she'd anticipated.

"Sixty percent," Henry said. Beads of sweat popped up along his hairline, pasting dark curls across his forehead. "After what, ten seconds?"

"I can't shoot the bastards if I can't see the bastards," Astra said.

"That's the idea," Iz said. "Maybe they want us alive." She ducked the ship beneath another huge rock, immediately swerving to the side as another came at her from below. What kind of disorganized cluster of rocks was this, anyway?

Not that she knew anything about the behavior of Verity's rings, or how its moons affected the gravitational pull of debris. Given the opportunity, Iz would have researched those things before diving in headfirst.

"Starboard," Henry said, and Iz banked away from a cluster of pebbles twice the size of the ship.

But the barrage of sand was unrelenting. It cracked into the shields like hail, dropping them to solid orange. Forty-five percent.

The minute they failed, there'd be rocks jutting through the walls.

"Don't want to get crushed into jelly today, Iz," Astra said.

But there wasn't anything to do about it. The rocks were everywhere, rushing around them on all sides. Closing in. Iz swerved, hands trembling. She couldn't fly through this. It was impossible. Iz wasn't a hero. She was just a moderately decent pilot who'd won a race or two and hated the idea of shooting other people out of the sky enough to take an unimaginable risk.

And now she was stuck. Iz lifted her hands off the dash. "Take the controls."

Henry didn't hesitate, which under the circumstances, Iz appreciated. Still, it felt like a failure. She was supposed to be the best pilot here, and she couldn't even fly under pressure.

Henry dipped the pod's nose around, looping back toward Verity.

The pod shot out of the rings and Astra adjusted the steering-wheel-like gun sights, lining up her aim on the screen in front of her. Easier to shoot green dots than actual ships with actual people on them, Iz thought. Enemies or not.

Astra fired, and the ship on their tail fell away in a spiral of gas and rapidly extinguished flame. Iz decided not to ask how she'd learned to do that.

The pod rocked to the side as one of Keyes's other ships

landed a direct hit to the hull. The shield bar on the dash dropped to red. Twenty percent.

"So much for wanting us alive," Astra said, lining up another shot.

Henry pulled the pod around, and Iz squeezed her eyes shut. There was something strange about battling out here. It wasn't silent—the pod's alarms saw to that—but even after all the space travel she'd done, it felt like there ought to be explosions and booms to accompany the quickly extinguished fire and shrapnel.

Henry spiraled the pod below the third ship. "Ready?"

Astra clenched her steering-wheel sights at ten-and-two. "As ever."

Henry pulled up, giving Iz a full view as Astra's missile crashed into the last ship's hull. The gunner split in two, wreathed in flame. Iz couldn't help picture the people inside, whoever they were, fighting to escape. Were they wearing atmo suits? Iz and the others weren't. If a missile had hit them, they'd have spilled unprotected into space.

Iz had not meant to sign up for this when she agreed to fly Astra back to SATIS.

It was supposed to be over.

Henry pulled the pod up and away from Verity's orbit. For a few minutes, everyone was quiet. Despite all her tough in-battle talk, Astra wasn't celebrating now.

Maybe she'd been expecting a few quiet weeks, too, especially considering her new relationship with Henry.

"Now what?" Iz said finally.

Astra laced her fingers together. "Maybe we can enjoy the victory for a second."

"Maybe we can set a course so the next ships don't know where to find us," Henry said.

"We shouldn't linger," Iz said. "It's how they snagged us on Verity."

Astra rolled her shoulders back, apparently unworried. She had her red hair rolled into a bun on top of her head, and even that looked pristine. Like she was on her way to the market. "Keyes just lost three ships. I think we can take a breath."

Iz didn't like to glare, but she found herself doing it anyway. Astra's way of doing things had landed them in this mess to begin with. "Keyes probably already has backup on its way. He's got resources we don't."

"Just a few," Henry agreed.

Astra sighed. "Well, we know Keyes got SATIS's love code. And for some reason he wants the SATIS girls. I think we should start with them."

"SATIS girls?" Henry echoed.

Astra sat back in her chair, stretching her legs out in front of her. Either space battles relaxed her, or she put on a really good show. "It's what I call them in my head. All the girls SATIS raised. Whatever. Fay said there was a rogue girl in Landry City."

"And we're supposed to trust a woman who tried to kill us," Iz said.

"Usually I'd say no. But Landry City happens to have a random vigilante type patrolling its streets at the moment. Coincidence?"

Henry frowned, made an adjustment on the control panel. "Isn't Landry City supposed to be one of the safest spots in Toccata?"

Iz nodded. "My family spent summers there. It is."

"Was," Astra clarified. "Crime's up by twenty-five percent this year."

"How much of that is because of this vigilante?" Henry asked.

"According to the news, she's only helped so far. Don't look at me like that, Henry. Fay says there's a rogue girl on Landry, news says there's a kickass vigilante on Landry. Our skillsets aren't exactly run-of-the-mill."

Iz wanted to point out that Astra hadn't known there were more women who'd been raised by SATIS until a few days ago. She refrained.

Henry guided the ship gently past Verity's largest moon. "Unless Fay was lying."

"She had no reason to lie."

Iz sat back in her chair and closed her eyes, trying to ignore their bickering. Henry had already set course for Landry City, which meant the conversation was more flirting than fighting, anyway.

They were remarkably calm after facing a battle in space. With ships and guns and things blowing up.

This was not Iz's territory. At all. The only thing she could do to help was pilot the ship, and her attempt to do that had almost gotten them killed. The energy-pumping adrenaline from the battle had drained, leaving her body shaky and raw. She wasn't meant to be a hero. She didn't want to be one. So why was she so disappointed in herself?

Maybe she should ask Henry to drop her on Marya. Dad would send a transport to pick her up. She could go home.

Or maybe she was trying to avoid Landry City, and Claire. And the ghost guarding her dressing room. The thought made her grimace. She'd been searching for Claire for five years. Now that she'd found her, she was making excuses not to go. Was she really so afraid of rejection?

"Don't worry," Astra said. "You'll get it next time. It was a fair plan."

Iz opened her eyes, confused, until she realized Astra was talking about her attempt to navigate the rings, not about Claire. Was Astra actually trying to be...nice? Well. They *were* supposed to be friends now. "Thanks? I think?"

"You mentioned you know someone in Landry City," Astra said, and Iz was grateful for the change in subject. Even if the change in subject was about Claire. She didn't particularly care to discuss her piloting failures. "Do you think they'll help us?"

Iz wanted to close her eyes again. She settled for looking at her hands, forcing them to remain still. "Let's go find out."

5

CLAIRE

Landry City was made of music.

Even on the outskirts of the city, snippets of song twisted into the air, given wing by curved towers that swept them skyward with the acoustic sensation of an ancient cathedral. The towers caught each note, each secret, and carried them to Claire Leroux's ears.

She perched beneath the hover-rail track that ran alongside the old Palais grounds, where she was tucked into an alcove that only her digital eye could have located. The arch was small enough to force her into a deep bend, her knees nearly brushing her cheeks. She'd waited in this position for almost an hour, joints aching for a stretch.

If Landry City was a cathedral, Claire was its gargoyle: hideous, powerful, and primed to protect her home.

The seven o'clock train whooshed above her head, vibrating the platform with a violent reminder that she had but half an hour to complete tonight's mission. Forty-five minutes at the most. After that, she'd have to return to the opera house or risk blowing her carefully constructed cover.

Half an hour should be plenty of time for a scouting

mission. As long as her quarry didn't stop for a hot pretzel on the way to meet his boss.

The train still hurtled by above, its passing a concern only because of the time. Claire's metal hand locked to the support poles, her shoulder bracing the rest of her body. Nothing short of an explosion would dislodge her until she allowed it.

A cyborg might not be able to find a decent apartment or walk undisguised through a crowd, but hey, she could cling to the underside of a hover-rail track without so much as breaking a nail.

The condition had its perks. Weird perks, sure, but perks nonetheless.

Including the ability to identify the man she was tracking from twenty-five feet in the air. He passed directly beneath her, heading straight for the main gates of the Palais grounds. He was a slight man, no more than a sliver of shadow. But recognizable, too, for the fan of hair arranged in careful spikes along the center of his skull. Clearly he'd skipped the section of his Henchman 101 course on making oneself indistinguishable.

And now, he'd lead Claire straight to his boss.

That was the important thing. The key, really. Because this guy just happened to work for the asshole who'd killed Claire's parents.

Claire unlocked her hand from the pole, replaced her glove, and gripped the wire she'd installed to swing lightly to the ground. She crept along the shadows and through the gates, using the old palace's plentiful trees for cover as twilight bruised Landry's sky, more of the planet's escort of satellites fading into view with each passing moment.

The Henchman had his hands balled into fists in the pockets of his sweater. It was too heavy a garment for a spring day that Claire's scent replicators indicated was packed with flowery perfume. He must be delivering something.

The Henchman took one last look at the quiet street behind him, missed Claire's tree-lined hiding place completely, and dove into the palace grounds as if those overly pruned hedges might offer protection.

They wouldn't.

Claire followed him, steadying herself as the usual Palais-induced headache poured into her temples. She'd visited the palace a few times before, for opera donor events, and every visit had been plagued by the same mysterious headache. It was definitely some kind of feedback, but from what sort of tech, she'd never been able to figure out. She'd sung in the music room, eaten in the dining room, and wandered among the strange sculptures in the garden—an old man surrounded by three ghostly figures, a girl peering through a garden hedge, five women in bonnets that made them look like satellite dishes—with a tour guide yammering about the ancient stories they represented, all while some unknown tech hammered at Claire's brain.

All she needed to do was to find where this guy was headed. Once she did that, she could ditch the headache, disappear into the opera house, and become another person for a few hours.

She'd return later to corner the Green Cyborg himself— the man who killed her parents—and she'd stop him from hurting the city she loved. Because he was behind Landry City's increase in crime. The break-ins, the muggings. She'd been tracking him for months.

The Henchman continued along the path, slower in the dim light of the palace park, where trees interrupted the ever-growing twinkle of the satellites. Candles glowed in the windows of the sandy brick palace ahead.

Claire crept along the grass to the Henchman's right.

Too easy.

As soon as the thought hit her mind, a shadow peeled out of the treetops, the motion calling Claire's attention a split second before the figure swung into her path.

"Hi there, cupcake," the shadow said. A woman's voice. "Road's closed."

On the path, the Henchman's footsteps slowed. Claire didn't bother trying to see her roadblock. She kept her attention on the Henchman, watching him as he stopped and turned toward the distraction.

Yeah. Henchman 101.

Claire feinted toward the shadow woman as though to attack, then swerved at the last minute and leapt to tackle the Henchman. If she couldn't follow him, she'd get him to talk.

The Henchman cried out in surprise and hit the ground with a dull thump. He was as slight as he looked, all bone and skin. As he struggled to land a punch, Claire slipped his precious delivery out of his pocket and into hers.

"Who do you work for?" she asked, avoiding his flailing arms. Claire didn't need a digital voice box, thankfully, but she'd had one installed anyway. It was helpful for moments like these.

Her voice was the quality she most needed to disguise.

The shadow from the tree slammed into Claire from the side. The woman was on her in a moment, pinning her to the ground.

"You must be the Angel we've heard so much about," the woman said. She was pale skinned, with the hint of an old scar whitening the corner of her eye. No mask, no makeup, no attempt to hide her features.

Must be nice.

"My boss is curious about you," the woman said, swiping for Claire's mask. Claire seized the opening and pushed her feet against the pavement, whirling the brunette to the ground. She twisted her attacker's hand away from her mask —not that the woman would have been able to remove it; only a command to her computer system could do that.

"Good," Claire said, "because I've been trying to schedule a meeting for ages."

"It's so tough to find a good secretary these days," the brunette said, voice strained as she fought Claire's attempt to pin her. Claire silently willed her to slam her head into Claire's—she'd be seeing stars for days—but the other woman twisted her hand easily out of Claire's grip and swung a fist for the unmasked half of her jaw.

Claire dodged. The brunette popped to her feet.

The woman could fight.

"You. Fourteen," she said to the Henchman, who was still lying dazed on the path. "Why aren't you running?"

Claire had hardly realized he was still there. Her sensors detected his elevated heart rate, the whitewater of adrenaline surging through his veins. She didn't want to let him get away, but she didn't have time to engage his protector, either.

Back through the gardens, the seven-ten train surged through the night. Twenty minutes to curtain.

"Is his name actually Fourteen?" Claire asked as the Henchman scrambled to his feet.

"I can't keep them all straight, and there's no point when half of them are just as ignorant as that one. Laser fodder, every one of them."

But not this woman. She stood almost casually, hands dropped to her sides, head tilted as though listening to the Henchman's receding footsteps. Claire could hardly hear them, which meant anyone without tech in their ears would be out of luck.

While she was thinking it, the woman flew at her. Claire grunted as their bodies slammed together.

Who was she?

The train roared behind them, and there was no doubt now. Either it was the seven-twenty, or Claire was completely screwed. She had to get out of here.

Her attacker swung a fist for Claire's throat, and Claire intercepted her wrist with her left thumb and index. "I usually fight fair," she said, apologetic, and while the question was still in the other woman's eyes, Claire sent a mild shock through her arm.

The woman staggered back, surprised. It wouldn't stop her for long, but it was enough for an escape.

Claire ran.

She bolted through the shadows, back through the palace gardens and straight to the arch where she'd hidden earlier this evening.

This time, she went underground.

THE TUNNELS beneath Landry City led lots of places, though Claire didn't often stray as far as the Palais. Still, she'd made it her business to know the way.

She was used to the transition from damp silence to musical madness as she rounded the corner that brought her directly beneath the bowl-shaped opera house and into the melee of sawing violins. And, predictably, the frantic voice of the music director.

"Where *is* she?" he said, plaintive, and Claire made a note to placate Firmin later with chocolate.

"She'll be here," someone said—a clarinet, maybe. Claire didn't hear his response as she hurried toward her dressing room.

The tunnels might be as old as Landry City itself, but the entrance to her dressing room was brand new. Before she slipped inside, she changed carefully out of her stealth clothing and replaced it with a dressing gown. She left the mask for last, unhooking it from her face with care and setting it reluctantly aside to trade it for her famous veil.

The mask was more comfortable. Safer. In comparison, the veil felt filmy and insubstantial. She hooked the ends under her chin and wove the long strands beneath her robe to hide the wires in her neck. The veil only looked floaty; the outer layers would catch the wind, but it was as solid as her mask, even if it didn't feel that way.

Ever since her operatic debut, veils had become something of a fashion movement in Landry City. The irony of it made her laugh.

When her transformation was complete, Claire found the latch she'd installed on the wall and slipped inside.

Sitting in the chair before her dressing table, back straight, hands in her lap, was a woman with the unmistakable eyes of Claire's childhood sweetheart.

Claire froze.

In her defense, Iz looked equally shocked. "Claire," she said, her voice hitting Claire's ears like a clear, warm song. More than her eyes, which might have been liquid pools of starlight, it was Iz's voice that had always betrayed her emotions. A tremble on the vowel, the way her Maryan accent made her linger on the L. When Iz spoke now, there was no question of what she was feeling: deep, complicated confusion.

What Claire felt, on the other hand, was far more diffi-cult to untangle. It was like the hot pain of circulation pulsing through a reawakened limb, relief and fear mingling until she could hardly tell one from the other.

Iz licked her lips, and Claire could almost predict her words before Iz spoke them out loud: "Did you just walk through the mirror?"

6

CLAIRE

S taring at Isabelle Chagny was like looking through a window to the past. Claire didn't let herself think of Iz. Ever. She'd learned the hard way that defining home as a person—or people—could only lead to heartbreak.

Claire wasn't Claire anymore. Not to Iz, not to anyone. She was Angelique D'Aae. Shaking off her shock, she clothed herself in the soprano's confidence. This was just another performance, albeit a private one.

"How did you find me?" Claire asked.

And how had she bypassed Claire's security system?

Iz's eyes flickered to the mirror behind Claire, her question hanging unanswered between them. There was a reason Claire dressed behind it; she'd anticipated one day opening the door to find someone waiting for her. She'd never imagined that person would be Iz. The one person she couldn't contemplate lying to.

Well. She was going to need to contemplate it.

"I found you by accident," Iz said. "I heard you sing."

That would do it. Iz was probably the only person alive who'd make that connection.

"I looked for you," Iz added. "For years."

Claire knew what Iz wanted her to say, the explanations she was hoping for. Why hadn't Claire sought her out? Why hadn't she found Iz again, if she'd survived the explosion?

Angelique wouldn't have cared about Iz's feelings. The truth was, Claire couldn't bear the thought of Iz's expression shifting to revulsion when she learned the truth: that her ex-lover was half machine now, and cared for nothing but vengeance.

But Iz's presence in her life would only be a liability. Claire needed to get her out of this room. Now.

There was no reason to hold back the truth, then, unless Iz decided to run screaming to the opera manager. Claire assessed Iz—her digital eye had no trouble seeing through the veil, and her organic one wasn't covered—as though she might learn who Iz had become in the last few years just by looking at her. Iz had the same soft curls springing around her ears, the same warm brown skin, the same spark of kindness in her dark eyes, though it was laced with hesitation.

Iz would recoil if she knew Claire was a cyborg. She'd be horrified, and she'd run from the room. But unless she'd changed beyond recognition, she wouldn't reveal Claire's condition to her employers. Or worse, the press.

If Claire did this right, Iz would simply leave and never turn back. The thought sent a dollop of lava spinning through her stomach, dread and hope mixing in a confused cocktail of emotions.

She cleared her throat. Firmin would have scolded her for that, probably. "A lot has changed."

"Sure," Iz said, twisting her hands in her lap, "you're a superstar now. There's even a ghost guarding your door."

So she had encountered the Opera Ghost after all. At least the illusion was still functioning. To Claire's knowledge, Iz was the only one who'd ever barged past it.

Well, fine. Not many people were as brave as Iz.

There wasn't any sense in drawing this out. Claire clenched her stomach and plucked the glove from her left hand in one smooth movement.

For a moment, Iz didn't stir. She sat there, hands in her lap, and Claire wondered if she understood what she was seeing.

Claire's hand was made of shining silver metal—aluminum alloy, specifically—with ringed joints and panels in the palm and wrist for tool and maintenance access. She hadn't opted to upgrade to any of the more humanoid aesthetics, preferring function over beauty. No fingernail dents, no lifelines. Certainly no skin or freckles or wrinkles.

Iz stood. To head for the door. To leave Claire behind forever.

That was the plan, after all. There was no reason for her stomach to boil over with pain.

But Iz didn't storm out. She stepped forward and reached up to cup Claire's organic cheek in her palm. Her hand was warm against Claire's skin, and she smelled like a garden. It had been so long since anyone had touched her with tenderness.

"That explains the veils," Iz said.

Claire whipped around and jerked her costume from its hanger, leaving Iz with her hand extended in open air. Claire's cheek tingled where Iz had touched her.

"You have to go," Claire said. She didn't know whether to be relieved at Iz's acceptance of her new body, or anguished at her failure to banish the stubborn woman. The rest of the system might cringe if they knew what she was, but Iz was not the rest of the system. Claire was a fool not to have anticipated that.

She ducked behind her changing screen to hide her confusion and leaned her hand against the wall, steadying her body against the crashing waves of emotion and allowing herself three breaths to pull her act together.

When she'd had them, she discarded the dressing gown to pull on her layered costume, made to correspond with her infamous network of veils, and waited for the door to open and shut.

It didn't.

"I need your help," Iz said.

It was unfortunate that the screen did nothing to muffle the beautiful melody of her voice. Iz spoke quietly, but even without seeing her face, Claire could tell she must have been desperate to come here.

How long had she known Claire and Angelique D'Aae were one and the same? How long had she waited to make her appearance? It had been foolish to hope she might have come here for the sake of a long-lost love.

And yet, the way she'd cupped Claire's face suggested otherwise.

"I don't know how I can help you," Claire said. She fumbled through the buttons on the side of the dress, the metal fingers clicking so fast it was a wonder they didn't spark.

"You're the only person I know in Landry City," Iz said. "We've heard—my friends and I, that is—that there's this vigilante roaming the streets. We need to find her."

Claire almost ripped the dress. There was no way Iz

could know. No way. "Everyone in Landry City knows about the Phantom Angel."

The words sounded too loud. Too defensive.

"We think she's in danger."

"Tends to be the case when someone leaps from rooftops and chases after criminals," Claire said.

She hadn't meant to become a full-fledged vigilante. As it turned out, tracking the Green Cyborg meant running into an increasingly violent web of crime, and no matter her own agenda, she couldn't just let his thugs snatch purses and hold up corner stores.

Not in her city.

Iz didn't laugh. "My friend Astra was raised by a corrupted artificial intelligence."

To anyone else—to the innocent Claire that Iz thought she was talking to—those words would seem like a bizarre non sequitur. To Claire, they made far too much sense.

It had been SATIS who'd saved her from dying after shrapnel tore her escape pod—and half her body—to shreds, SATIS who'd directed the hospital to outfit her with cyborg parts despite their disgust, SATIS who'd taught her to fight and kill for the sake of her messed-up tragic backstory.

And it had been SATIS who hadn't thought it was worth chasing the man who'd murdered Claire's parents when she found him running a petty crime ring in Landry City last year. He wasn't an anti-AI radical, and he wasn't Edward Keyes. So SATIS didn't care.

Which was why Claire worked alone now.

Could SATIS have sent Iz here? Could this friend of hers be the woman Claire had encountered in the park? Her fighting moves had been so good. When Claire thought about it, some of them felt eerily similar to her own training.

Claire stopped trying to button the dress and stepped out into the dressing room.

"We think this AI raised a lot of girls in the same way," Iz continued, clearly unfazed by Claire's reappearance. "May I?"

For a moment, Claire didn't understand. Iz gestured to the unfinished buttons.

Claire tried to breathe. It was harder than it should have been. She nodded.

Even with so many layers of silk and lace between them, Iz's touch electrified. "We think your vigilante is a SATIS girl," Iz said, her voice soft.

"Sounds like a band name."

Iz laughed. Claire's chest ached. "It's what Astra's been calling them. It was kind of a shock to her, learning that her AI mother had dozens of other daughters out there. Including—we think—this vigilante of yours."

"And what, this AI wants to find her or something?"

Claire wasn't planning to go back to SATIS. Not quietly. Not even with Iz. She'd been lying to herself, pretending that pushing Iz from her mind would keep her heart safe from harm. Now that Iz was here, touching her, speaking in that haunting voice of hers, Claire felt like she was a few dangerous breaths away from collapsing into Iz's arms.

Good thing half her skeleton was made of metal. It kept her on her feet.

Iz finished the buttons, her touch lingering for what felt like an extra moment before she stepped back. "The AI is dead. But the girls are in danger. If you can—"

"Sorry," Claire interrupted, her thoughts catapulting between *the wicked AI is dead, good riddance* and a twist in her stomach that knew she herself would be dead without SATIS's intervention.

If danger came her way because of her history with SATIS, she'd handle it. "I can't help you," she said.

"But if you could just—"

"The Phantom Angel might care about this...SATIS thing, but I don't know where to find them. And I don't care."

It took everything she had to keep her voice steady and her eyes cold as she swept toward the door, dredging up every ounce of Angelique D'Aae's hauteur. Angelique was a lie, but she was a safe one.

She'd let herself be Claire Leroux for far too long.

"Thank you for the buttons." She tossed the words back over her shoulder, like an afterthought. "If you're still here when I return, I'm calling security."

7

CLAIRE

Firmin was practically spinning the place into a tornado by the time Claire made her way upstairs. He held his baton in one hand, his tuxedo tails threatening props and stagehands with every move he made. He was a nervous man at the best of times—whenever he wasn't immersed in music, really—and Claire's absence had him whipped into a panic.

"Angelique, you miscreant," he said, his voice half hysterical. "Where have you been? Carlotta is poised to take the stage on your behalf. And with the Canon System ambassador in the audience!"

Behind him, Claire's understudy was already shedding a costume identical to Claire's, handing off bits of lace and silk to a stagebot whose tray was piled with prop candlesticks. If Carlotta was jealous at the change in plan, she didn't let on, though certainly the tabloids did their best to concoct a rivalry between the two singers.

Claire never bothered to try deflecting it. There wasn't a point, especially since she suspected Carlotta might even court the drama. Claire hadn't made a point to get to know the other singer, and even after several months in the same company, they were practically strangers.

Claire laid a gentle hand on Firmin's arm. "I'm sorry, chérie," she said, lacing her voice with all the sugar she could and trying to compose herself. Iz had her completely undone. "I needed an extra hour of preparation this evening. My hair is a disaster."

Firmin wrung his hands, distraught. He was opening his mouth to blather something more when someone else spoke up from the wings.

"Your hair is a revelation."

Claire hadn't seen Monsieur Andre overseeing the chaos from the wings, but if Carlotta was being discussed, the opera manager would of course be the one to make the ultimate call. He nodded when Claire's eyes fell upon him, and she half expected a lecture.

The first thing Claire always thought when she saw Monsieur Andre was that he was too handsome. His nose was too straight, his lips too ready to smile. The trouble with handsome men was that they often knew exactly how handsome they were.

Luckily for Claire, she was immune to that sort of thing. From men, anyway.

At least Andre was not merely handsome. He was capable, too, his short tenure at the opera already transforming it from stale staple to glittering sensation.

"I'm relieved that you're in good health, Mademoiselle," Andre said. "Perhaps next time you might consider updating Firmin as to your location."

"For the good of all in his path," Carlotta put in, tossing a string of beads at the waiting bot.

"Of course," Claire said.

Andre leaned in closer, bringing with him a whiff of

spiced cologne. "I realize time is short, Angelique, but would you be willing to greet a patron briefly? I'd be most grateful."

Half-dressed, Carlotta snorted. "If only the Phantom Angel would show up and save us from fundraising."

Andre's expression didn't flicker. "I doubt he troubles himself with such matters."

"I'd be happy to speak with the patron," Claire said quickly, eager to move the conversation away from the city's much-talked-of vigilante. "It's the least I can do."

Andre beamed. How he could be so calm with Firmin quivering not three feet away, Claire had no idea. "Wonderful," he said, lowering his voice. "I hate dancing for donated coin, but alas, it must be done."

The elderly woman who tottered out of the wings wore one of the more elaborate veils Claire had seen, a tri-color array she'd attached to a ruby red hat. "My granddaughter," she said, as though continuing a conversation, "came to Landry City last month—she's from Novem, you see, tiny little backwater, I keep telling them they should—well, I brought her to the opera, and she simply loved it, and— well, would you be able to give me your autograph? For Lucy?"

The old woman said all of this in a single rush of breath, veils trembling.

Claire smiled, trying to tuck her anxiety behind her. "Of course. I'm glad your granddaughter enjoyed the opera."

"Oh, she was absolutely stunned," the woman said, handing Claire a leather-bound notebook. "I've been collecting mementos in here, of our trip. As a gift. Your signature—well. She'll be thrilled."

"What a lovely idea," Claire said, and it was. It made her own heart ache, to think of them together.

She didn't allow herself to think of Iz, and she certainly didn't allow herself to think of family.

"I wish I could bring her back for Gala Night," the woman said. "You will be singing, won't you?"

Claire laughed. Gala Night was the only thing Firmin cared about these days. Aside from her punctuality. "I will definitely be singing."

"I want you to know," the old woman said, "I've added the opera house to my will."

When Claire hesitated, unsure of how to respond, the woman chuckled. "Oh, don't you worry darling. I don't act like it, but I've got plenty to spare. Why do you think your Andre invited me here tonight? Oh, yes, the opera's accounted for. Don't you worry."

Claire blinked, unsure of what to say. "That's very generous. I hope we won't be seeing those funds any time soon."

The old woman took her by the arm, her nervousness apparently washed away. "A diplomatic response, my dear. Now your music director looks ready to burst. Perhaps I'll see you after the performance."

Claire allowed herself to be led into Firmin's world, still feeling a touch off balance. As he ushered her into the wings, she caught Carlotta's eye, and the other singer touched a hand to her eyebrow in a little salute.

The whirlwind of the opera swept her into its thrall. Claire tried to forget about her encounter with Iz, to lose herself in the music that was her only anchor, but she sang every heartsick aria with memories of young love in her chest, and real tears wet her cheeks as the hero mourned her death in the finale.

All the times she'd thought of what she'd say to Iz if they saw each other again, all the explanations and histories, the truths and the memories, and Claire had said none of it.

She'd been too shocked, too bruised from her fight in the park, too inundated with surprises. She wished she'd remembered at least a snippet of it. But in truth, that would have been an unkindness. Claire had nothing to offer.

Besides, Iz had come here to ask a favor. That was all. There was nothing left between them. Not that Claire would have encouraged her to stay, anyway, but it would serve her well to remember exactly what Iz had said, and why she claimed to have come.

When Claire returned to her dressing room after the last notes of the encore, Iz was gone.

Claire sighed. Why her heart should feel empty at Iz's absence after Claire had basically threatened to have her arrested—or at least bodily removed—was anyone's guess. Hearts were not to be trusted, in general.

She was undressed for the night, her costume re-hung and her room tidied, before she remembered she'd taken something from the Henchman. Between the chase, the fight, her lateness, and long-lost sweethearts popping up out of the ether, she'd forgotten.

Claire locked the door to her dressing room before sliding back through the mirror. That was a creation she was particularly proud of; she'd watched herself appear from the hidden camera in the ceiling, and the layers of reflective glass she'd installed around the rotating door really did make it look like she was floating inside it. Not necessary, exactly, but fun.

The stolen item was still in the pocket of her folded vigilante costume, a cylindrical data file that fit neatly into the port in the back of Claire's head. When her system finished its safety checks and allowed the information to filter into her eye, she smiled.

She hadn't missed the main event, after all. The file was

a meeting request, apparently too sensitive for the sender to trust the networks. Of course, whoever it was should not have trusted their most clueless Henchman, either.

It looked like Claire was about to have a chance to tell him that. In person.

Even better? The mysterious new crime boss of Landry City would be holding his next meeting on Claire's turf.

He was going to be here. At the opera house.

8

SAM

S am let himself into his aunt's apartment and staggered straight to the freezer, hoping she kept ice on hand. His lip was split and swelling, his cheek throbbing. His jeans were ripped at the knee where he'd fallen on the gravel, and he had no idea how he was going to buy new ones. Especially if he got fired after tonight's screw-up.

He was just supposed to be an errand boy. He wasn't supposed to get ambushed by the freaking Phantom Angel while delivering a data file.

Sam popped an icecube out of a neon-green tray and collapsed at the kitchen table, wincing as it touched his lip. He always felt like a smudge sitting in Aunt C's cheerful kitchen, with its pink accent wall, plants in the window, and music-note magnets holding inspirational quotes to the fridge.

He hadn't been sitting there five minutes before the lock on the door beeped, and his aunt entered in a bustle of bags and chitchat. Aunt Carlotta came into every room like a thunderstorm. Or maybe a one-woman band.

"The new ballet dancer entered from the wrong wing tonight," she said-slash-sang, switching on the apartment's news holo as she passed through the living room. She loved to fill her home with layers of background noise, constant streams of chatter over music over more chatter. She had no trouble flitting around or holding conversations without paying attention to any of it.

Sam, on the other hand, could never fully tune out the babble of voices. He tended to get pulled in. But Aunt C had given him a place to stay, and he didn't feel right complaining.

She bustled into the kitchen and set her bags on the counter without glancing at him, removing containers that smelled like chicken and peanut sauce, with a tang of something peppery. "The dancer almost crashed into the tenor, and there was nearly pandemonium, but then—Sammy, what happened to your lip?"

This, she said half turned, her lips parted in surprise. They were still stage-red from the performance. She'd scrubbed the rest of her makeup and pushed her blonde hair back with a cloth headband, but a hint of sparkle still lingered along her lash line.

"Nothing," Sam said, his voice muffled against the ice. "Work accident."

The news holo flashed blue against the walls of the other room, the correspondents discussing the disaster at the Star Leaders Academy last week. Someone had succeeded in taking over the VIP tour ship's AI, and they still didn't know exactly what had happened, so the talking heads were batting theories around.

Aunt Carlotta set her fists on her hips. "I'm not sure I like the type of work you're doing."

"I'm just a gopher," Sam said.

"A gopher with a split lip. What's your boss's name? Maybe I need to give him a call."

Sam tried to picture Aunt Carlotta scolding The Cyborg for getting her nephew injured. He wasn't entirely sure she'd lose that fight. "I don't know his name."

She leaned back against the counter and scrunched one eyebrow, her way of compensating for the fact that she couldn't lift just one. It was something they'd laughed about before. Now, it was just annoying. "You don't know your boss's name? I know you're young, so I'll help you out here. Don't work for someone who won't tell you his name."

Sam's cheeks burned. Carlotta wasn't even a decade older than he was. "I'm not a kid anymore. I'm eighteen. You told me to get a job, so I got one. And now it's not good enough?"

"Not if you're showing up at home with a split lip."

Home. This wasn't home. It was just a potpourri-smelling imitation. He didn't want to stuff his head into a top hat and work at the opera house as an usher, or take on any of the jobs she'd offered to get him there. Sweeping floors. Running props. It wasn't for him. No, Sam wanted to prove his father was wrong to call him a worthless leech, to make something of himself. On his own.

Aunt Carlotta pulled a pair of plates out of the cabinet and set them emphatically beside the takeout containers. "I'm just going to say it. Your boss is creepy. Ditch the job."

"He's not creepy," Sam said, but he wasn't defending his boss so much as his own choices. The Cyborg *was* creepy, with that green mask, and that computerized voice. So was the Phantom Angel. He'd always thought the system had the right idea, keeping an eye on what amped-up humans could and couldn't do. By the time he accepted the job and figured out who his boss was, it was too late to back out. A cyborg could probably track everything about him with the literal blink of an eye. Set him on fire or something. So Sam told himself the job made him feel like a badass, and he stuck with it.

The blue-tinged talking heads were discussing the future of the Star Leaders Academy in the other room. Would it reopen? Was this the end? As if anyone but gossip-mongers gave a shit about what happened to Star Leaders brats. If the school closed, something else would pop up in its place.

People like that were born with opportunities, while people like Sam scraped by with bloody lips and nagging aunts.

Aunt C set a plate in front of him like he was a ten-year-old in need of serving. "I just want the best for you. If it takes time to find the right job, then it takes time. You can stay here as long as you need."

In other words, she wouldn't kick him to the curb the way her deadbeat brother had.

Sam shoved the food away and got up, the chair scraping loudly on the tile. "Not hungry."

Aunt C popped a bite of chicken into her mouth and wiped her lip with a napkin. "I'll save you some leftovers."

Sam waded through the glow of the still-babbling holos in the living room and left the apartment, slamming the door behind him.

9

ISABELLE

I z had to hike across half the city to reach the port where Astra and Henry were hiding in the pod. On her way to the opera house, she'd been so full of antic-ipation and hope that she'd bypassed the hover-rail in favor of the lively feeling of the streets, where the city was busy and sparkling. People had hurried out of hotels and resi-dences alike, heading for Landry City's famed music halls. The opera house might be the crown jewel of the city, but the music that spilled through open doors as the downtown drew nearer demonstrated that even the smallest theaters could promise a good show.

People whirled around her, dressed in brightly colored sundresses and feathered fedoras, the light from Landry's ever-present satellites catching on sequined clutch purses and elaborate belt buckles. Laughter and perfume mixed in the air, and it had felt to Iz like she was walking through a kaleidoscope.

The return trip to the spaceport felt quite different. The streets had all but emptied, the people tucked into their theaters and showrooms of choice. Music and laughter still chased her down the street, but it was muffled now.

It ought to have been dark, but Iz had visited Landry City often enough to be familiar with the constant twilight glow of the satellites, beaming so brightly overhead. Some moved, like a continual show of shooting stars. Others appeared frozen.

Gems on the ground. Gems in the sky. Iz could see why Claire loved Landry City.

As for Iz, she wished she could risk calling her father. Not to ask for help, as much as she craved it, or to assure him of her safety—as much as he likely needed that. She'd messaged him from Verity, so at least he knew she'd escaped from the *Traveler*. What would he think, if she failed to contact him again?

She wanted to hear his voice, and to weep. He was the one person who would understand her heartbreak.

Never in her imagination had Iz thought Claire might receive her as she had tonight. Cold. Uncaring. Had she truly thought Iz would judge her for what she'd become? That Iz would hold such a thing against her? Iz knew how cyborgs were treated in the Toccata System. She wasn't naive, or ignorant.

And Iz might be far from perfect, but Claire should know she objected to mistreatment of *anyone*, cyborg or otherwise. It hurt that she didn't. Hadn't Claire stood by Iz's side while she told off strangers for kicking pigeons by the canal? Hadn't they wondered, together, whether AIs ever wanted vacations, or career changes, or hobbies? It wasn't the same, not exactly, but it was related. It was relevant. Five years shouldn't have erased any of it.

Iz crossed the river via the Glass Bridge in the center of the city and headed straight for the hover-rail station ahead.

The spaceport was sprawled out beyond the tower-lined riverbank, in a section of town where rooftops reached for more modest heights.

Here, the crystalline sidewalks turned to mundane concrete. The walls became mere stone, as if a spell had been broken. Though Landry City's downtown still sparkled behind her, Iz didn't turn to look at it.

Astra and Henry were seated crosslegged on the floor when Iz opened the hatch, a deck of cards spread between them. They looked up, expectant, as Iz collapsed into the pilot seat. Astra had her red-orange locks tied in a messy bun on top of her head, wispy strands falling around her pale white face.

They'd been sleeping on the floor of the pod, packed together like sardines. The ship was starting to smell like a tin of fish, too. Iz grimaced, wondering if she'd carried that smell with her to see Claire.

Again, she wished she could reach out to Dad. It would be so easy for him to help—the famous hero pilot would descend to the rescue in an instant—but Keyes would likely be watching him, and Iz wasn't going to risk her father in all of this.

"Dead end," Iz said.

Astra sighed. Iz hadn't told her the nature of her relationship with Claire, but Astra had been there when Iz returned to *Traveler* with Jane after the disastrous revelation at the opera. She had to know there was more between them than Iz had been willing to admit.

"I'm sorry," Astra said.

"So," Henry said, drawing a pair of cards from the center stack, "we lie low for a week or two. Try to find this vigilante ourselves. It would've been good to have a lead, but we didn't really expect it."

"It's one card, not two," Astra said. "You still suck at cards. I think we should go to Eding."

At that, Iz sat up in her chair. Henry looked up, frowning, as if Astra might just be saying that to distract him from the game.

"It makes sense," Astra said.

"I thought we wanted to find this vigilante, since you're so convinced she's a SATIS girl," Henry said.

"I am," Astra said. "She is."

"Keyes will look on Eding first," Henry said. "We shouldn't be seen there."

What Keyes wanted with SATIS girls, they had no idea. But they did know that he wanted to control the system using SATIS's corrupted code, so preventing him from recruiting a band of trained assassins seemed like a good idea.

"Eding is full of criminals," Astra said. "We'll blend right in."

Iz tried to picture gentle, clean-cut Henry blending in with criminals. If she hadn't just had her heart stomped on, she might have laughed. Not that Iz would blend any better.

Astra probably could.

"We should stick to the plan while we're hidden," Henry said.

Maybe Claire had merely been surprised to see Iz. It had been more than five years since their last meeting, and that conversation had not ended well. Claire probably thought that Iz hadn't bothered to search for her.

But Claire seemed impossibly certain, and Iz forced herself to remember that Claire was the one who hadn't bothered to look. After the transport disaster, she'd simply disappeared. Mom and Dad had tried to convince Iz that Claire was gone, but when she dug in her heels, describing the staticky radio call she'd received right after the explosion and insisting that Claire had to be alive, Dad had sighed and agreed to help.

Even with all of his contacts, all his resources, they hadn't been able to track Claire down. A young teenage girl, alone on her own in the Toccata System. She shouldn't have been difficult to locate. Where had she been?

She'd been injured, clearly, either in the disaster or in the years since. Transformed into a cyborg. As beautiful as ever, though. Even her speaking voice was like a song.

Astra was saying something about hiding in a crowd of pirates and thieves, and Henry was saying something about the way Eding probably smelled—which was hardly a deterrent, considering their current circumstances—but Iz barely heard the conversation. She kept replaying the scene with Claire in her mind. Something felt decidedly off about the whole interaction.

Once Iz had asked about Landry City's vigilante, Claire had studiously avoided her gaze. It felt wrong. Suspicious. Iz hated to apply that particular term, but on the other hand Claire had entered the room *through* her mirror. Yes, she was a cyborg, and yes, she needed to hide that fact if she wanted to avoid public derision—let alone keep her job. Still, something about it felt off. As if Iz had stared straight at the answer and yet missed it entirely.

"I'm going to try again," she heard herself say. She had a feeling she'd interrupted the argument, that she'd spoken right over Astra, but only because the other woman's mouth was still open as she stared at Iz.

"Are you sure?" Astra asked. "I'm not— Is she worth it, Iz?"

Iz took a deep breath. Claire was worth it. Iz didn't hope for reconciliation, not anymore. She wouldn't ask for it, not after she'd been rebuffed. But she wasn't entirely sure that Claire was safe in Landry City, and until Iz was certain, she couldn't leave.

Besides, she still needed to contribute something positive to their situation. Iz wasn't a fighter. The least she could do was get some information.

"I think she knows more than she's saying," Iz said. "I'll go back tomorrow night, after the opera. If she doesn't know anything, we can go to Eding."

Astra threw Henry a triumphant look, as though the vote had been decided. Henry just sighed and muttered something about pirates and halitosis.

Iz spun the chair toward the window, the only measure of privacy she could hope for in such close quarters. Astra and Henry resumed their card game, and Iz stared out the window, glad that the garage door hid the sight of Landry City and all its glittering pain.

10

CLAIRE

The Landry City Opera House was as much a place to network and ogle celebrities as it was to actually listen to music—a fact Claire tried not to take too personally.

Especially since it made the opera house a clever meeting spot for people who otherwise presented themselves as disconnected. From her vantage on an abandoned limb of the lighting catwalk—abandoned mostly because of the work she'd done to brand this area as haunted—Claire had seen notes passed between secret lovers, money slipped into tuxedo pockets, boxes and cards and capsules exchanged with wrist flicks and flirtatious smiles.

Unless her attack last night had altered her enemy's plans, he'd be doing business here as well. After years of searching for her parents' murderer, she still didn't even know his name.

Tonight, she'd see his face.

Claire crouched on the pace-wide grate, leaning through the safety bars to watch as the last few stragglers wandered out of the opera house. She waited eye-to-eye with the famous chandelier, a modern jumble of crystal cubes that were lit from within by electric candles. It looked as if it were meant to evoke earlier times while also springing forward with the new.

Iz had always liked the chandelier. Claire thought it was ugly as hell. The woman had plagued her mind all night, memories rushing through Claire's dreams as though through a broken dam.

The feelings would pass, and if they didn't, she would make them. She had to. She couldn't afford to get distracted. Iz was gone. That was that.

As the audience trickled out of the auditorium, the Henchman from last night inched into the hall. He held the door for a woman in a crimson gown, half bowing as she thanked him for his politeness. Not awkward at all, guy. Not awkward at all.

Whoever the boss was, he either didn't mind that the Henchman had botched last night's delivery, or he was so short-staffed that he couldn't afford to care.

These details could be crucial.

As she watched the Henchman bob his head at the retreating woman's back, the door at the other end of the arc swung open. Claire tensed.

It was Iz.

Claire whispered a curse as Iz slipped through the door and headed straight for the front of the opera house. It was a long, sinuous route through the bowl-shaped auditorium, and she walked like she was on a mission, curls bouncing against her shoulders.

Of course Iz would show up here, now. Even after Claire's rebuff last night.

Claire had half a mind to fulfill her promise of calling security on the damn woman.

The man who was about to show up here tonight? He was dangerous. If Iz was around when he made his appearance...

Cursing to herself, Claire moved away from the safety of her catwalk and toward the main paths, where quick-footed lighting technicians might still be poking around. She held her grapple at the ready, in case she needed to swing above someone. The lights still radiated heat from tonight's performance, and Claire made sure to avoid brushing them in her rush to reach Iz. The determination in Iz's steps was all too familiar, even after so many years. Iz thought of herself as quiet and shy, and others might think her unassuming. But when the woman wanted something?

Watch out.

Claire raced along the catwalk, aiming to intersect Iz's path before it was too late. Metal legs would have been a great asset right about now. Loud, maybe, but fast.

A door banged open, back toward where the Henchman had been standing. Claire didn't dare look. Inhaling, she secured her wrist-grapple to the railing with a solid throw. She waited until Iz passed behind one of the thick cubic columns, then dropped through the shadows to clamp a hand over her mouth.

Before Iz could squeak in surprise, Claire swung them both up to the catwalk and released the grapple.

As soon as their feet hit solid metal, Iz started fighting Claire's hold. Understandable, but dangerous. She was strong, if untrained, and Claire had to wrap an arm around her to keep her from thrashing—or throwing them both off the catwalk—then switched off her voice box and leaned into Iz's ear. "You're safe. It's me."

Iz froze. Claire waited a beat. Let the words sink in. Her organic cheek pressed into Iz's hair, the strands silky against her skin. She could feel Iz's chest heaving, see the strain in her throat. Some wild part of Claire's mind begged her to drop her lips to the delicate patch of skin below Iz's earlobe. Instead, she let go.

Iz whipped around, the light from the chandelier sending shining highlights through her hair. Her cheeks were flushed.

She was luminescent. Claire's throat went dry.

"I knew it," Iz breathed.

Claire raised an eyebrow, though all the motion did was to rub her skin against the inside of her mask. If Iz wasn't going to be shaken by Claire's transformation into a cyborg, or her current status as Landry City's vigilante, Claire couldn't think of anything that might rattle her.

"You knew I was the Phantom Angel?"

Iz gripped the rail, darting a look toward the ground as if she'd only just realized how high they were. "No, but I thought you knew more than you were saying. What are you doing here?"

"Working." She lifted a hand to her lips, and Iz stopped talking. Though she was still staring at Claire with that open, surprised look on her face.

Another person might have glowered. Accused. Iz just looked...curious.

So much for keeping things simple.

Well, Iz was here now. The safest spot in the opera house was by Claire's side, so she might as well carry on with her mission. Claire took Iz by the hand and led her along the catwalk, slow and silent. When they reached the supposedly haunted limb, Claire crouched to wait for her enemy, pulling Iz down with her.

She'd lost precious moments by swooping Iz out of danger's path. Not that she regretted it, but it still meant she had to catch up with the progression of events. The Henchman still stood by the doors, shifting his weight every few seconds and gnawing at his nails. She hadn't missed the Green Cyborg's arrival, but then again, it wasn't impossible that the data file had been a plant. A red herring, designed to distract her—or anyone else who tried to track it. What if the boss never showed?

Claire shoved those worries aside. For now, the data file was the only lead she had. They'd stay hidden, Claire would learn what she needed to learn—or resign herself to another dead end—and then she'd get Iz out of here.

Nothing good could come from staying close to Claire. Her mission meant chasing danger. Regularly. Intentionally.

Claire realized suddenly that she was still holding Iz's hand, and she pulled away, heat rushing to her organic cheek.

Below, the Henchman straightened abruptly and opened his door with a deferential nod. The man who stalked in didn't so much as spare him a glance.

Claire knew him.

Apparently, Iz did too. She hissed in a breath. "You're spying on Edward Keyes?"

Not intentionally. As much as she'd wondered about the Green Cyborg's identity, it had never occurred to her to suspect Keyes. Claire had spent three years with SATIS; she knew the face of the man who'd broken the AI's heart. Not that she particularly cared about that drama, especially not now, but he did look like a bastard on a mission. Still, it didn't make any sense that he'd have been the one to kill her parents. He was an important figure in the Toccata System, to begin with; he was a leader, an authority in the field of artificial intelligence. If he was a cyborg, he had no reason to be angry about it.

Motivations aside, Keyes didn't seem tall enough, or broad enough, to be the Green Cyborg. His shoes looked too fussy and shiny to be hiding metal feet.

Claire couldn't picture this finicky man fighting with any degree of success. But then, who could picture Angelique D'Aae as a masked vigilante? That was the point of a secret identity. And memory was notoriously faulty.

"He chased us off Verity after SATIS died," Iz said. "He's the one...he's after the SATIS girls. He wants to use SATIS's corrupted code to control the system."

There was a beat of silence. Claire pressed her lips together, trying to reconcile her memory of the Green Cyborg with the villain of SATIS's past.

"Does this mean you really are a SATIS girl?" Iz asked.

Claire didn't respond. She didn't know how. Iz clearly knew what it meant to belong to SATIS, the kinds of monsters the AI produced. Perhaps becoming a cyborg wasn't enough to convince Iz of the kind of person Claire had become. But working for SATIS? That left no room for interpretation. SATIS had trained assassins. As far as Claire knew, only Viv had managed to evade that particular job description.

Luckily, the Henchman opened the door again, and just to make it a party, the next person to arrive was the brunette who'd attacked Claire in the park. Dark as it had been, and strange as the angle was now, her identity was clear. She stationed herself at the doors as if the Henchman couldn't be trusted—she wasn't wrong about that—and waited, straight and tall, muscular. Scowling. Not to be trifled with.

"I guess Fay took Keyes up on his invitation to form an alliance," Iz said quietly. "She loved SATIS like a mother. Why would she do that?"

Claire couldn't help it. She swiveled her head to look at

Iz, reassessing the woman. Maybe Iz was more familiar with danger than Claire gave her credit for. "Who *don't* you know?"

On the stage, the curtains parted.

A figure stepped out. His green mask glowed, the rest of him silhouetted against the dim stage lighting behind him. Claire caught the murderous glare of one of his metal feet, her sound sensors registering the heavy tap of his walk.

"Him," Iz breathed. "I don't know him."

11

CLAIRE

C laire's head swam, her vision tilting and righting itself as the Green Cyborg loomed like a giant on the stage, his eyes flashing the same electric red as they had five years ago.

She took a deep breath, swallowed hard to keep from vomiting. "He killed Mom and Dad," she said, almost without meaning to. She was gripping the railing so hard she was surprised she hadn't crushed it. "He took down the transport."

Iz gasped, and the sound of her shock nearly defeated the last of Claire's defenses. But she couldn't afford to be sad now. She had to pay attention. This Green Cyborg had killed her parents. And now he was wreaking havoc on Landry City. Claire needed to know why.

It was disappointing that he'd shown up in disguise, but interesting, too. He was working with Keyes while keeping his identity secret. That had to be useful information.

Who worked for whom? Or were they partners?

Keyes reached the front row and stopped, tilting his

head up slightly to look toward the stage. "You know I dislike meeting in person."

"As do I." The Green Cyborg used a voice box, and his words reverberated through the acoustically perfect theater. Claire hoped all the stagehands had left for the evening, gone on to drink or sleep. She knew what the Green Cyborg would do if he came across one of them in the dark. He'd murdered a transport full of innocents right in front of her, and in the years since her return to Landry City, he'd proven he thirsted for more than revenge. Every mugging she'd stopped, every robbery she'd prevented, she'd traced back to the Green Cyborg.

He didn't care who lay bleeding on the street, or the catwalks, as long as he got what he wanted.

Her eyes flickered to Fay. The woman still stood at the doors like a soldier. Watching.

"There are some things best discussed face to face," the Green Cyborg added. Ironic, Claire thought, considering his was hidden.

"Such as my waning faith in you," Keyes said.

All right then. Keyes was the boss.

"No need. The plan is underway."

"You have the hover-rail heart in hand?"

Iz gasped again, and Claire stifled the urge to clap a hand over her mouth. Maybe she ought to. The woman's emotions were far too open for subterfuge, and the acoustics in the hall were too good to trust. She scanned the figures below, heart kicking up as she dug her fingers— metal and organic—into the grating of the catwalk. She'd run, if she had to, but it would mean a major loss.

This was the moment she'd chased since her return to Landry City. This was her chance to take her nemesis down before he knew she was coming.

No one glanced up, and Claire let herself relax enough to consider what Keyes had said. The city's hover-rail system was operated by an artificial intelligence, of course, and like every AI it contained a "heart"—a physical object that could be reset, or even destroyed if necessary. The heart was an AI's failsafe. Its center.

Claire didn't know where Landry City's AI hearts would be stored. In a vault somewhere. Under lock and key.

She'd need to find out.

If SATIS had listened to Claire a year ago about the Green Cyborg, they could have stopped this plan. Had SATIS known the man's connection to Keyes? How could she *not*?

The Green Cyborg tapped a thumb against his hip. Claire's digital eye caught the movement, which on him felt like the equivalent of shifting feet or a blush on someone else. She wondered if he was contemplating a lie.

"I will." His footfalls were heavy as he strolled toward the edge of the stage, and Claire found herself wondering if he'd rehearsed his speech, blocked out his movements. "The plan is underway."

"You ought to have procured it months ago."

"No," the Cyborg responded. "If the hunt is called too early, the rest of the plan will collapse."

Keyes stood almost directly below him now, at the lip of the orchestra pit. His expression was hidden by the strangeness of the angle. "If your obsession with revenge causes you to fail, I will not be forgiving."

"He has SATIS's love code," Iz whispered. "Do you think his friend knows that?"

One more revelation, and Claire's circuits would overload. What the hell did he mean to do with SATIS's love code? And what was he waiting for?

She didn't dare respond. One stray sound, and they'd be discovered. Claire lifted a finger to her lips, silently begging Iz to comprehend the danger they were in. She wasn't prepared to face the Green Cyborg. This might be Claire's turf, but he had backup. If he discovered them now, she'd have to fight him. And she might not win.

The Green Cyborg was quiet for a long moment, as though he had questions, too. "The heart will be difficult to extract," he said finally.

He seemed ready to elaborate, but Keyes was already producing his tablet from his pocket. "How much?"

The Green Cyborg named a number, and Keyes tapped on the screen. When he was finished, he reached into his pocket and withdrew a small silver box, the details of which were obscured by the distance. Claire zoomed in with her left eye, but it still just looked like a box. "I'll leave you with some extra insurance."

"What is that?" the Green Cyborg asked.

Keyes stepped forward and set the box on the edge of the stage. "An invention of my son's. I've made a few modifications. My associates will send the details on a secure network."

Keyes turned to go, then stopped to flick something off the back of one of the seats. "Don't screw it up."

"It's Conor's AI jammer," Iz said, her voice trembling.

Claire frowned. Did that mean Keyes's son was evil, too? Iz's tone suggested otherwise. Questions crowded into Claire's mind, but she silenced them. She'd get the full story later. She couldn't begin to guess how sweet, innocent Iz could have gotten mixed up in all this.

Without so much as a wave goodbye, Keyes headed back up the aisle. The Henchman opened the door again, and Fay followed Keyes out.

So Fay was lapdog to Keyes, and the Henchman worked for the Green Cyborg—whose task was to procure the heart of the city's hover-rail AI for Keyes.

But why? What profit could there be, in any of it?

The Green Cyborg still stood on the stage, completely motionless. She wondered what he was thinking about. Was he relieved that Keyes had given him the funds to continue his project? Worried that Keyes might return? Still hovering by the doors, the Henchman fidgeted with the hem of his shirt.

"Little pests," the Green Cyborg said, his tone mocking. "I see you."

For a moment, Claire thought he meant Keyes and Fay.

And then he pointed up. Straight at Claire and Iz.

Claire's heart kicked up like an ignited engine. She ignored the fearful twinge of her stomach, her old wounds long healed and stitched. She'd spent a year haunting his footsteps, calculating her every move. One moment, one slip, and all her efforts cascaded out from under her.

She wasn't ready to face him. Not yet.

She had to get Iz out.

Claire leaned into Iz's ear. "Run."

Before Iz could respond or object, Claire secured her grapple to the grated floor and swung down into the theater. She wasn't ready to face him, but she had to if she wanted to buy Iz the time she needed to get away. She'd just have to trust Iz to navigate the catwalks on her own.

The Green Cyborg remained on the stage, his expression unreadable behind that emerald mask. The mask shifted color with every step Claire took. From the catwalk, he'd looked big; down here, it was obvious how massive he was. He loomed over the auditorium, and Claire had to admit it was impressive that Keyes hadn't showed so much as a hint of fear.

"You take a vested interest in my work, Angel," the Green Cyborg said as Claire zipped her grapple back into her shoulder and stalked down the aisle toward him. She hoped he couldn't make out the hammering of her heart. "And yet I don't believe we've been introduced."

His voice box made him sound like rolling boulders, grating and crashing together. She could hear the rattle of metal above as Iz ran. She hoped Iz was doing as Claire had said and escaping to the street. And that the Green Cyborg hadn't brought enough backup tonight to chase her down.

Hope. It was never enough.

A duo of thugs came running toward Claire from either side of the stage, one with hair as long and pull-able as Claire's would be if she didn't pack it away for her disguise, the other wearing crimson red sneakers that flashed across the floor as he ran.

Like the capital-H Henchman she'd come to know and love, these two were unmasked.

And that was all she had time to note before Red Sneakers came within kicking distance. Claire landed a blow to his jaw, and he bounced into the wall of the orchestra pit with a satisfying grunt before crumpling. "I could see those shoes from space," she said.

The other henchie was steps away, blond hair streaming behind her. Claire spun, ready to defend.

And then the woman's head wrenched back, her hair caught in someone else's fist.

Iz's face appeared over her shoulder.

So much for following instructions. The henchwoman ducked her head and easily twisted around to lock Iz's neck in a hold.

Great. Claire swallowed a wad of panic.

It was disconcerting how the Green Cyborg simply stood on the stage, watching. As though to study Claire's moves, or see how the situation would play out. Maybe he knew something she didn't—that there were a hundred other thugs on their way, or guns ready to fire out of the light fixtures. The thought was unsettling.

"Let her go," Claire said, and the henchwoman bared her teeth. Iz still had her hair wrapped around a wrist, tilting her captor's head at an awkward angle. Claire suspected the woman would be visiting a hair salon for a nice pixie cut before she found herself in another fight.

The Green Cyborg still watched, still as a statue.

Claire launched herself at Iz's captor, sending them both stumbling. Claire's titanium-and-aluminum skeleton made her heavier than she looked. She used the woman's upset balance to twist her arm away from Iz's neck and shove her roughly away. Iz landed in one of the front row seats, arms splayed, and Claire hit the other woman across the throat with her metal hand. The woman tried to retaliate, but Claire dodged and took her down with a good hit to the back of the skull.

The Green Cyborg chose this moment to leap down from the stage, sailing over the orchestra pit to land heavily in the aisle.

Claire dove for Iz, who still looked dazed. She scooped her out of the seat and tossed her toward the stage. Iz caught the edge and scrambled up, and Claire silently thanked her for her trust.

The Green Cyborg was still aiming for Claire. He'd overshot his landing—perhaps on purpose, to demonstrate his power—but he moved quickly. Another few seconds, and he'd be on top of her.

She wasn't equal to fighting this hunk of metal. Not today. She had to get Iz out of here, and only she knew the way.

Claire scrambled to her feet and took a running jump, using the wall of the orchestra pit to launch herself onto the stage. That was mere calisthenics, no alterations needed.

She grabbed Iz's hand and pulled her behind the curtain, to the center of the stage. Before the Green Cyborg could follow, she sent a command to her system.

The floor dropped out beneath them.

Holding onto Iz's waist, she fell.

12

ISABELLE

Iz clung to Claire as the floor pulled them under, the theater lights giving way to complete darkness. Their feet hit the floor perhaps five feet down, enough to smart through Iz's thin shoes—but surely not far enough to be secret. Not like Claire's stunt with the mirror.

Iz didn't know much about theater, but she'd seen Claire rise from beneath the stage when she was here with the Academy.

"Hold on," Claire said. Before Iz could ask whether she meant to wait, or to physically hold on—which Iz was already doing—the floor opened again.

And now they were sliding. The passage wasn't completely vertical, but it was steep enough to pull them faster, faster, through a mine-dark tunnel where gravity dragged them down, down, far longer than should have been possible.

Iz doubted that the stagehands knew about this part.

The tunnel dropped away.

Claire landed on her feet, all grace, and steadied Iz before she could tumble to her knees.

Iz supposed, dazedly, that Claire must do this a lot. She put a tentative hand out and felt for the wall. It was smooth as polished stone, and close enough that she was glad not to be claustrophobic. The air felt cool and damp. Cavelike.

A latch clicked—Claire must be able to locate it with her digital eye, because Iz could see nothing in the disorienting dark—and Iz braced herself for another fall. Instead, Claire led her through the wall.

The corridor on the other side had dim sconces hanging haphazardly from the ceiling, wires twisted and cobbled. Iz almost expected to see sparks.

Instead, the lights flared, and Iz gasped as the room widened to reveal a hundred more fixtures arranged along the ceiling in a checkered patchwork. The space must be enormous, despite the feeling of close walls. She reached out a hand, tentative, her eyes still on the lights. It brushed the wall. Glass.

Mirrors.

Iz dropped her attention from the fire-hazard lighting to find dozens of copies of herself, a dizzying multitude of identical images that made her want to sit down and drop her head into her hands.

Maybe it was just the long fall. Or the fight with the cyborg and his friends. Or the sight of Edward Keyes, the man who'd terrorized Iz and her friends off Verity.

There was a lot to contend with at the moment.

"What is this?" Iz breathed.

"Security," Claire said, her voice grim.

Iz touched the wall again. "How is this security?"

Claire glanced at her—Iz saw it in the mirror—and Iz thought there was a spark of amusement behind that mask of hers. "Would you like to try to find your way out?"

It was clearly a rhetorical question, but Iz tipped up her

chin—dozens of mirror-Izes did the same—and took a step forward.

The other Isabelles moved toward her, like a dance.

Iz made it three steps before she walked into a wall.

Claire had the grace not to laugh. Instead, she edged past Iz and turned right, slipping directly into an image of herself and continuing on.

Iz would have sworn there was a wall there.

She followed behind Claire, staying close at her heels. The air smelled musty, but with an undercurrent of sweetness—lilies, she thought, though that felt so incongruent she almost laughed out loud.

What disconcerted Iz most about the new Claire was not the metal or the computers. It wasn't even the twisted mirror-hallway security, or the vigilante status, though Iz certainly had a question or two about those choices. No, what worried her was the silence.

Iz had tried to tell herself over the years that when she found Claire, her friend—*friend*, she reminded herself firmly—would be different. That whatever had happened to keep her from contacting Iz must have been enough to change her in a deep way. Perhaps even a traumatic one.

Knowing that intellectually was one thing. Facing it—this silence from the woman who'd spent her childhood singing—was an entirely different matter.

When Claire finally stopped, Iz couldn't have said why. She couldn't have picked out what was special about the mirror where Claire inserted her ring finger into an invisible slot, like the world's strangest key.

Iz would not have wanted to get lost by herself here. Which, she supposed, was the whole point. In all her life, she'd never paid so much attention to the opening of a door.

Claire's hand disappeared into its reflection. The lock clicked. The door swung wide.

There was a lake on the other side.

Not a water tank. Not a koi pond or a long forgotten ornamental fountain. An actual body of water, like they'd stepped out into the middle of Landry's countryside. The surface was as still as the glass in the mirror hall, and a single spot of light burned across the distance, casting its glare across the water like a searchlight. Iz couldn't make out the source, or the opposite shore—an island, perhaps.

An underground lake. Why not an island, too?

Iz took a breath and tried to understand. The ceiling soared out of sight above, and her lightheadedness returned for a moment as she tried to picture their position relative to the opera house. She was completely disoriented.

Off to the right, Claire tended to a small rowboat, untethering the craft and shoving it toward the shore. "Are you coming?"

Iz looked again to the light on the water, her mind overflowing with mirror mazes. This Claire was a stranger. She fought like Astra. She lived alone in the middle of an underground lake.

But this Claire had also saved her tonight. This Claire couldn't mean her any harm.

Iz stepped into the rowboat and took up the oars. "You did the fighting. Let me do the rowing."

Claire grinned and relinquished the oars. "Fair enough." The warmth in her voice made Iz's throat squeeze.

Iz used the oar to push off from the shore, sending a parade of ripples to foretell their coming across the lake. For a few minutes, there was only the sound of the creaking boat, the water sloshing as the paddles met the surface. Iz headed for the distant light without instruction, and Claire did not correct her.

"We thought the Phantom Angel was a SATIS girl," Iz said after a while.

Claire swallowed, tapped her fingertips on the side of the boat. "I was. She made me a cyborg." Her fingers tapped, tapped. "The rest were adopted much younger. Most of them."

Claire had known there were others, and Astra had not. Iz thought of Fay, of how odd it was that she'd shown up here tonight. And working for Keyes, who had been SATIS's enemy. There were as many variations to the story as there were girls.

"Did you feel SATIS die?" Iz asked. She wasn't sure if 'die' was the right term for it, but the AI's heart had been destroyed. It felt appropriate.

There was a long pause. Claire stared off across the water as the light grew ever closer. Iz could make out the shadow of a building beneath it now.

"No," Claire said finally. "I left her a year ago."

Iz wanted to ask why, but something in Claire's tone closed the conversation. For now.

Five years, they'd been apart. Five years of searching, of wondering. What had Claire endured during that time, while working for SATIS? Iz wanted to weep for her. She suspected Claire wouldn't thank her for it.

Iz rowed silently, enjoying the feel of piloting the boat. And the feel of Claire's presence, no matter the circumstances. The mask she wore was worked in delicate spirals, set with pearls and ebony stones. It was almost as beautiful as she was.

After what felt like hours, they reached the shore and

Claire hopped out, pulling the boat in so that Iz could avoid soaking her shoes.

The building before them was no larger than a hut, or a small cabin. Claire led Iz inside, where she lit a fire in the pit at the center of the room. A stone hearth surrounded the fire, complete with a chimney to chug the smoke into the vast cave. Firelight spread to illuminate spare wooden furniture, a narrow cot in the corner, blankets strewn about. A collection of cooking pots, a kettle, and various tins that Iz assumed contained food.

At the far end of the room, taking up the entire wall, was an organ.

Claire went for the kettle and filled it from a faucet before setting it on a hook above the fire. "The organ does better down here than a piano would," she said. "A lot of humidity."

"Of course," Iz said. Why shouldn't there be an organ on an island at the center of an underground lake that one accessed via a maze of mirrors?

"It's not easy for a cyborg to find housing," Claire answered, as though sensing Iz's unasked question. Questions. "The opera had no trouble hiring me in my disguise, but landlords do background checks. I couldn't risk it."

Iz thought of the house Claire had lived in with her parents in Landry City, next door to the vacation home Iz's family had rented every summer. Their windows had been matched, eave to eave, and from girlhood they'd passed treasure back and forth, stretching their arms to share dolls, seashells, drawings, and, later, love notes.

After the disaster, Iz had waited in that window while the rest of Landry watched the atmosphere incinerate what was left of transport A90D. With the sound of that staticky breathing in her ears, Iz had waited for Claire to appear, mechanically eating the food Mom brought at intervals, telling herself that when Claire returned, she would need Iz to be strong.

Now, Iz drifted toward the hearth where Claire was preparing the tea. "The other girls are in danger. Keyes is after them. We're not sure why, but he does believe they killed his son."

Though in all honesty, Iz wasn't sure Keyes cared very much about poor Conor's death.

"They probably did kill him," Claire said. "We're assassins. Remember?"

"You're not."

"I was. I killed people."

Iz swallowed. Fine. Claire had ended lives. Who had SATIS targeted, besides Edward? Would Claire tell her if she asked—and did Iz want to know?

It didn't matter, she decided. Claire was saving people now. "We need to help them," Iz said.

There was something funny about watching Claire prepare mugs of tea, masked as she was, her hair secured out of sight.

"I know," Claire said.

Iz startled. She'd been expecting more of an argument.

"But you heard the Green Cyborg tonight," Claire continued. "You heard Keyes. I can't leave my city in danger. He already took my parents. I can't let him take Landry City, too."

And Iz couldn't ask her to.

Claire poured the tea, the herbs staining the water with berry red, and handed it to her. "What if we help you first?" Iz said.

Claire looked up, and Iz thought it was her turn to be surprised. "You'd do that?"

Astra wouldn't be pleased to have a deal made on her behalf. But if she wanted Claire's help, she'd have to acknowledge the need here. Besides, they'd still be dealing with Keyes. Maybe they'd have a chance to take him out. That would help the girls, even if it delayed finding them.

"Of course," Iz said. "We'll stop whatever plan they have to hurt Landry City. After that, you can help us find the girls."

Claire stood and brushed her palms on her pants, assessing Iz. Then she extended her hand.

Iz hesitated.

"Come on, shake," Claire said. "It's good business, right?"

Business. Of course. Iz took Claire's hand, electricity singing along her skin as their fingers clasped together. Claire had held her hand on the catwalk tonight, pulled her close as they fell through the maze. This felt somehow more intimate. They were alone together, with no other sign of humanity within singing distance.

Claire grinned as they shook. Whatever connection Iz felt it was clearly one-sided. Claire was all business. "Looks like we've got a deal."

13

SAM

With The Cyborg's hired guns off nursing their wounds, Sam found himself patrolling the passage directly beneath the stage with his boss. Red-tinted backstage lights illuminated control panels and gears, and the ceiling was dotted with trap doors, performance drone modules, and dumbwaiter boxes for lifting props. He knew from his aunt that most productions used some form of pyrotechnics, and the sharp smell of ignited gunpowder hung heavy in the poorly ventilated passage.

It was hard to believe the Phantom Angel would be hiding down here. They'd been up and down the tunnel a dozen times, Sam rapping on the walls, The Cyborg's computerized gaze scanning for anomalies.

"Maybe they just ran away," Sam said.

He'd seen the woman run from Fay in the park. She was fast.

The Cyborg didn't respond. Probably because it had been a supremely unhelpful thing to say. There were guards posted at all the exits—guards she hadn't wounded—and none had seen her.

In any case, Sam had some respect to win back. Or win in the first place. He was murky on his original standing in the organization, but tonight's display of cowardice hadn't helped him any.

It didn't matter what his aunt thought. Sam just needed to keep this job.

Maybe they'd missed a stage door. Or one of the guards had snuck away for a cigarette. Sam didn't see any evidence of hidden passages back here.

Still, The Cyborg moved slowly through the passage. Scanning. Scanning. He was taller than Sam by nearly half a foot, and he had to stoop to walk through the tunnel.

When The Cyborg reached the end of the passage, he opened the door that led back to the stage and clomped up the steps. Sam followed, casting a final glance behind.

"Either she's installed protections against scans, or she left another way," The Cyborg said when they reached the stage.

What would happen if someone caught them right now, hanging out in the system's most iconic landmark after dark? Just chillin' on the stage, no big deal. The Toccata System's most famous diva had been standing right here tonight. The heartthrob tenor, over there. He'd have expected to run into cleaning staff sweeping the stage, or a stray ballet dancer who'd forgotten her shoes, but there was no one in sight.

Just as well. The Cyborg would probably rip an opera security guard in two. He didn't seem concerned about the risks of trespassing. He stood in the center of the stage, staring out toward the audience. He almost seemed amused.

"At least we know one thing about our new self-proclaimed nemesis," he said. "The girl has a weakness."

Sam blinked. If that tornado of a fighter had a weakness —other than Fay—he hadn't seen it.

"The woman with her," The Cyborg said. "She was desperate to save the woman with her."

Was Sam meant to answer? He glanced behind, to see if one of the more important employees had entered.

They were alone.

Maybe this could be an opportunity to be noticed. To say something worth remembering. There could be advancement opportunities, after all.

Sam cleared his throat. "But do you think she overheard your plan? About the heart?"

Sam didn't know The Cyborg's plan, precisely. Only that it involved procuring the heart of the hover-rail from its vault. Not legal, sure—he wouldn't have told Aunt C about this part, even if his job was still a welcome topic—but how bad could it be?

"Yes," The Cyborg said slowly. "Yes, I do think they heard. And that gives us an opportunity." He clenched his gloved hands together so hard that Sam expected to hear them creak. "We're going to set a trap."

14

CLAIRE

C laire's introduction to her SATIS sister was not off to a brilliant start. At least as far as she could tell, given that she was currently half eavesdropping on Iz's conversation with Astra while standing wedged between the spaceship and the rickety garage door of the dock. So far, all she'd heard was "you made a deal without me?" followed by the rise and fall of explanations.

She could have turned up her sound sensors, but she figured some arguments were best left unheard.

The pod was barely big enough to fit three people for a flight, let alone double as accommodations. Although, a cyborg living in a moldy underground cabin was perhaps not one to talk.

Claire had changed into her undercover diva uniform so they could make their way here using regular old streets rather than tunnels. The sparkly-masked vigilante thing wasn't going to cut it in the daylight, even the early dawn, so she'd traded that costume for soft flowing pants, long sleeves, and lace gloves that itched her biological hand like crazy, topped with one of her signature layered veils.

Ever since half the women in Landry City started copying the veil thing, strolling the streets unrecognized had become much easier. If they suspected what hid behind all that fabric, they'd be less inclined to imitate her.

It was a complicated feeling, to love a place that would shun her if it knew what she really was. Sometimes she imagined what it would be like to reveal her machinery in the middle of a performance and have the city embrace her with love and open arms instead of revulsion and horror.

Landry City was the symbol of light and progress in the system, the artistic capital. If hope didn't exist here, it didn't exist anywhere. The odds might be slim, but she had to believe it was possible.

Maybe one day she'd risk it.

Maybe.

Dawn lit the open sky above the dock, the last of Landry's satellites blinking out of sight in the glare of Toccata's morning arrival. Claire let herself close her eyes for a moment, allowing the rays to warm her face as the voices inside the pod dipped to whispers and rose back up again.

It wasn't exactly how she'd pictured reuniting with Iz, battling an evil cyborg before escaping to her damp little cabin, but Iz hadn't seemed to mind. She was either too polite or too captivated to comment on the strangeness of it.

Claire wasn't sure which she'd have preferred.

"Fine," Astra's voice said from inside the pod, responding to something Claire hadn't caught. "I'll hear her out."

Claire grinned. That sounded like her cue. She pushed away from the door and hopped up the short ladder into the pod.

Claire still wasn't big on spaceships. She was a Landry girl, through and through. The last time she'd left here had ended in...well, computerized parts and a murderous AI guardian, not to put too fine a point on it. She'd dealt with space travel over the last five years, but she still didn't like hurtling through a deadly vacuum while protected by a tin can.

Her sensors indicated that this particular tin can smelled like a gym, though someone—Iz?—had sprayed a hasty haze of perfume in the air. Something minty. Claire could still see the molecules of moisture evaporating into the space.

She turned down her scent sensors.

Iz stood with her hands folded at her waist. The woman beside her was tall and pale-skinned, with a muscular build and crop of flaming hair twisted on top of her head. The famous Astra. Raised by SATIS, like Claire, but from infancy.

Claire hadn't heard a man's voice chime into the conversation while she waited outside—which gave her a good first impression of the guy who sat calmly in the pilot's chair with his legs crossed. Of a tanner complexion than Astra, he had a cap of brown curls spilling over his forehead.

He looked ready to accept whatever conclusion the women came to. Claire wondered if they gave him much of a choice.

"This is Henry," Iz said. "And Astra."

She was practically wringing her hands, her teeth worrying at her bottom lip.

"Iz agreed to help me," Claire said. "You two can do what you want."

Astra assessed Claire with a level look that almost made Claire wonder if she had scanners installed in at least one of her eyes. There was something uncomfortable about it, but Claire returned her stare.

Displaying weakness to someone raised by SATIS would be the opposite of a wise move.

"All right," Astra said, finally, "we did come to help SATIS girls. Iz says you're one of them. Us. So what do you want?"

"Your welcome-committee speech could use some refining," Claire said.

Henry snorted.

"OK," Astra said, painting a friendly smile on her face with eerie ease. If Claire had walked in just then, she might have thought they'd been discussing this season's trends in sequined leggings. "Darling SATIS girl, what might we help you with? Before you'll agree to, you know, rescue dozens of other women from immediate peril?"

Iz looked like she might jump in, but Claire gave her head a shake. She appreciated the thought, but she needed to settle her ground with Astra from the beginning. "I want you to stop calling me a SATIS girl, to start," she said. "I ditched that bossy computer a year ago."

"Lucky you," Astra said, but there was something in her eyes that belied her flippant tone. Could that be...she wasn't actually grieving for SATIS, was she?

Why not? A part of Claire's mind whispered. *Maybe SATIS saved her, too.*

Saved. Ruined. When it came to SATIS, the difference was in the split of a hair.

Astra might expect people to obey her commands, but Claire wasn't used to following anyone's rules. "Iz and I heard the Green Cyborg's plan," she said.

"Keyes's plan, too," Iz put in, and Claire nodded. Emphasizing Keyes's involvement had to help convince Astra.

"They're after the heart of Landry City's hover-rail

system," Claire said. "I don't know why, but we need to get to it before they do. We need to move it to safety."

She expected Iz to chime in again, to agree. Instead, she exchanged a glance with Henry, who'd been mostly silent up to this point.

"You want to move it?" he asked. "Why?"

Claire blinked at him. "You heard me, right? City in danger? Hover-rail heart at stake? You can't tell me that someone trying to gain control over a major AI system like that is up to any good."

"With Keyes in the mix, that's a guarantee," Astra said.

"Maybe he wants to test the love code on it," Iz said. "See what it does with a large system."

"Does it matter?" Claire asked. "Bad guy. Powerful tech. Bad combo."

Iz still had her brow furrowed, thinking. Astra looked unimpressed.

Maybe she was used to being the bad guy. Claire could relate. But Claire had chosen to walk away from AI-induced murder and mayhem. If her motivations had been selfish, it didn't alter the outcome. Or so she told herself.

The spaceship was starting to feel too small, the walls far too close. Could Claire really leave Landry City in this thing? Trust it to deliver her safely to solid ground again?

A deal was a deal. But then again, Claire was adept at hiding. She might save Landry City and disappear. Cower underground until Astra and co gave up and left without her. Iz would never forgive her, but did it matter? They were doomed, anyway.

Claire shifted her weight and immediately regretted the show of weakness. She'd been working alone for too long.

"OK," Henry said. "But in any case, moving the heart is the last thing you'd want to do."

The more he talked, the less Claire liked him. "Why?"

It was Iz who responded. "Landry City unveiled a state-of-the-art AI-heart vault a few years ago. They have more AIs running the city alone than all of Verity and Eding combined."

Well, yeah. Verity was all strawberry patches and beaches. Eding was infested with criminals. Not as much need for AI administration, by a long shot.

"The vault is a maze," Henry added. "It's impossible to get through."

Claire considered fact-checking this revelation with her network access. It didn't seem likely. "I think I would know about that."

Iz shook her head. She knew how much Claire loved Landry City, and yet she didn't seem surprised at Claire's ignorance. "They premiered it while you were off world. They said..." She paused, wedging her bottom lip between her teeth. It might have been Claire's imagination, but she thought there might be tears in Iz's eyes. "Some people claimed it was an AI malfunction that caused the A90D transport disaster."

Fire spiked through Claire's chest, as it always did when someone mentioned the transport, phantom screams waiting in the wings of her memory to break into her mind. She ignored them. "That's a lie."

"Of course," Iz said. "But Landry City didn't have any leads, so they responded with this public campaign to protect its AI hearts. To appease people, you know? You were... You would have missed it."

Because she'd been with SATIS. "So you're saying they protect the most valuable and dangerous artifacts in the city with puzzles?"

It sounded like an elaborate story devised by the

Chamber of Commerce to increase tourism.

"With labyrinths," Iz said. "No AI oversight, no guards."

"It's kind of a famous thing," Henry said.

Astra shrugged. "I never heard of it."

"You didn't know AIs had hearts at all until a few days ago," Henry said.

That was interesting. Raised by an AI, ignorant about AIs. Though knowing SATIS, Claire could see why the overbearing computer might have kept her heart a secret. Couldn't risk a pissed-off toddler chucking it out an airlock because she wanted more juice.

Besides, Claire had been raised in Landry City, loved it more than anything, and she didn't know about this maze-labyrinth situation. She'd been a little preoccupied with her own affairs lately. Maybe Astra had, too.

"The point is, no one's getting past the security," Iz said. "The mazes are impossible to crack."

"That's great," Claire said. "Are they cyborg proof?"

Iz's eyes widened.

"Do you know how hard it was to cyborg-proof the route to my lake?" Claire asked. "Cyborgs can x-ray shit. Detect heat signatures. Scan for anomalies. It's expensive and time consuming to protect against us. Also, you'd need to hire a cyborg to help, and no one wants to do that."

The others looked around at each other, speaking in the secret glances of those who'd been sleeping shoulder-to-shoulder and breathing each other's sweat for a week.

Claire waited.

"I don't know if the mazes would be cyborg proof," Henry admitted finally.

"I doubt it," Iz said slowly. "There aren't that many cyborgs in the system. The extra expense wouldn't be worth it."

"Plus, they'd be bragging about it," Henry added.

Astra had been following the conversation with her arms crossed. Claire didn't know if these three functioned as a democracy or a dictatorship, but she suspected Astra's vote would carry a lot of weight.

If Astra decided to leave Claire on her own, would Iz stick around? Or would she go, too?

Astra said, "How do we know whether any of that is true?"

Iz startled, eyebrows raised. "Astra, she's—"

"Practically a stranger," Astra said. "Even to you. How do we know a cyborg can do all that?"

Claire crossed her arms, mimicking Astra's stance. So that was how her SATIS sister wanted to play it? Fine. "You've got a half-healed wound behind your left ear," she said. "Something SATIS installed there, right? I can see where the wires were. It's ragged. You ripped it out, or someone did."

Astra blinked. Henry shifted in his chair.

"There are four non-standard compartments hidden on this ship," Claire continued. "Henry's sitting on one, cut into the pilot's chair. There's another under Astra's feet, which I'm guessing is why she's standing there. Two more in the ceiling."

Henry swiveled his chair back and forth, fidgeting. "Can you see through our clothes, too?"

Claire couldn't tell whether he was joking. She could activate x-ray vision, if she wanted to, but that particular superpower took more energy than she typically liked to expend. Her movements recharged her power supply—she wouldn't have wanted to plug into a generator every night just to keep walking—but a few minutes of operating x-ray vision always drained her stores, forcing her to revert to the backup power buttons installed between her vertebrae.

Luckily, she had other fancy tools. Astra's wound was still flaming, making it easy to pick up on the heat signature in her head. And Claire's computer system could target anomalies in the make of the pod, allowing her to guess about the locations of hidden compartments and such.

But what fun would it be to tell him all that?

"Could," Claire said, winking. "Luckily, I don't care to."

Henry paled, and for a moment Claire regretted showing off her abilities. There was a reason people weren't entirely comfortable with what cyborgs could do. It was like Astra had said; these people were practically strangers. Even Iz.

Astra looked at Claire for a long moment. Not one to make quick decisions, this one. "Who is this guy?" she asked finally. "The Green Cyborg? Why's he working for Keyes?"

He killed my parents. He's after my city. "I don't know," Claire said. "I'd like to find out."

Astra nodded. "So would I. We'll help you defeat your Green Cyborg. And after we do, you'll help us find the other girls."

If the thought of leaving Landry City made Claire's stomach twist, it was nothing compared to the terror of facing this threat alone. She needed a crew. The price was fair.

Swallowing her relief—and the terror that came with it —Claire managed a grin. She could always change her mind.

She could always disappear.

"Great," she said. "Where is this maze-labyrinth thing?"

"That's an easy one," Iz said. "They keep the hearts on the outskirts of the city. At the Palais."

PART 3

ARIA

15

CLAIRE

M usic trails through the crack of window she's left open, lazy piano chords mixing with tinkling bells, the pull of a bow across fiddle strings. The combination is discordant, but pleasant. Familiar. Downstairs, Claire's parents drink country wine and laugh softly, assuming she's asleep.

But Claire is waiting for the shuffle and creak, the breath of air that will mean her window is opening. The anticipation of Isabelle's legs tangled with hers. Soft hands. Softer lips.

"Tell me," Iz will say between kisses, "how was your day?"

And Claire will tell her everything.

The window never opens. The breeze never stirs. Instead, a melodic alto voice chimes into Claire's head while she trembles beneath the covers, unable to move as the left half of her body is shaved away. Blood gushes out, a cascade, until wrenching metal twists and clicks into her bones. Claire can do nothing to stop it.

"I made you," the AI says. "I will protect you."

CLAIRE WOKE WITH A START, the dream fresh in her mind.

Dreams were rare since her transformation. She never knew if the computer prevented it, or if there was some other explanation.

And this was why she didn't mourn the loss. When she did dream, her memories blended, the painful poisoning the pleasant until she could hardly tell the difference anymore.

Claire swung her legs over the side of the narrow bed and pushed herself to her feet, forcing her body to move to the makeshift kitchen for a glass of water. There were still hours left before she was meant to meet the others for their venture out to the Palais. She had to make it through Gala Night rehearsal first, and she'd need her strength to maintain her Angelique D'Aae persona.

But she wasn't going back to sleep. Not with the hope of Iz's lips still lingering in her mind, the bitter disappointment of SATIS arriving in her place.

Claire took the water to her window.

She knew it was a strange choice to erect a house like this underground, beside a forgotten lake where rats roamed unhindered and natural light never reached. Claire hadn't thought much about it; she'd retreated underground when she left SATIS, hoping the AI would quickly lose track of her whereabouts. Either she'd been right, or SATIS hadn't tried.

She'd felt lucky to find this spot. A little stretch of shoreline, a lake for plentiful water. Ink-black water, yes, and it had to be triple boiled and purified before it was drinkable, but still. It had its own kind of beauty. The silence was complete, with just enough of a breeze from outside to ripple the surface of the lake.

She'd thought it was beautiful. A cyborg with a lake house. It shouldn't have been possible.

And yet...and yet, when she'd brought Iz here yesterday, when she saw the reflection of this place in Iz's eyes, Claire saw how lonely it truly was. How completely still. How strange.

Claire sipped her water, wishing for a jolt of something stronger. She didn't dare drink a drop of alcohol before executing a plan; it went to her head too fast, messed with her circuits. She'd never been much for drinking, so she didn't mind. But sometimes a swallow of liquid courage could go a long way.

Claire finished her water and retreated from the window to wash her cup. She needed to make it upstairs in time for gala rehearsal.

After that, she'd prepare for battle.

THE OPERA FINALE surged around Claire in a kaleidoscope of color and sound as the last chord reverberated into the empty hall. Usually, the curtain would sweep shut at this point, sending the cast scurrying for encore positions. But this was the Gala Night dress rehearsal, which meant feedback and adjustments and possible repetitions.

Not too many, she hoped. They had to wait until nightfall to search for the AI hearts, but it was hard not to be impatient, to leave Astra and the others to scout the location and gather supplies. The longer Claire lingered here, the more time the Green Cyborg had to get ahead of her and take the AI hearts himself.

She wanted to get going.

It didn't help that some costume designer had decided to crown Claire's veil with a puff of feathers. They kept dipping haphazardly toward her cheek, and though she couldn't feel them tickling her skin, it was a concentrated effort not to let the headpiece fall.

As if she didn't have enough to focus on, memorizing full opera libretti in ancient languages no one even spoke anymore. She had to balance feathers, too.

The last echoes of music faded into the auditorium, followed by a beat of silence.

In the orchestra pit, Firmin burst into tears. With the lights in her eyes, Claire could make out only his quivering silhouette. "It's perfect," he sobbed. "A masterpiece. My flowers. You're stunning."

The stage lights dimmed, bringing the rest of the hall into focus. They had guests tonight, a group of Andre's donors. He'd seated them in the front row, and Claire caught sight of the grandmother she'd met the other night, looking slightly disheveled beside her impeccably dressed neighbors. The old woman lifted her hand in a small wave.

Firmin had tears on his cheeks, and he couldn't keep his hands still. He kept passing his baton back and forth between them. "This Gala Night will be the talk of the system for a year."

In the front row, Andre cleared his throat. "Why don't we call for notes, Director?"

Carlotta sidled up beside Claire and offered a hand to help her down from her platform, which Claire accepted gratefully. Why they had to begin and end with her tottering in midair was a mystery.

They'd dressed Carlotta with a tiara made of feathers, too, though hers were much smaller. Claire wasn't sure she understood the theme. Were they supposed to be parrots?

"Notes?" Firmin said. "My dear Andre, you heard that performance. I hardly think it's necessary to—"

"With respect to your direction," Andre interrupted, "I would like to demonstrate to our opera friends—"

"—aka moneybags," Carlotta whispered, and Claire covered a laugh. But despite her quip the soprano was frowning, her usual energy dampened.

"—that the Landry City Opera is committed to excellence," Andre finished, projecting his voice over the murmurs of the cast and the insulted sputters of his music director.

"*I* provide excellence," Firmin huffed.

"And," Andre said, "that we are willing to embrace modern technology?"

Firmin dropped to his conductor's stool and crossed his arms, clearly unwilling to let an anyone else—even, or perhaps particularly, an artificial intelligence—tell him how to improve his art.

Because that was what Andre meant, of course; one of his first moves as opera director had been to install an AI to assist with the artistic side of the opera.

Claire didn't mind one way or the other. She didn't have a problem with AIs in general. She'd had a problem with SATIS. Judging them all based on that experience would make her just as bad as the people who judged all cyborgs based on the actions of people like her green-masked friend.

That was most of the system. Claire refused to be like them.

She leaned back on her platform beside Carlotta, waiting for the AI to pipe up with notes. The other woman was worrying her ruby lip between her teeth, a decidedly un-Carlotta-like expression.

"Everything OK?" Claire asked.

"Oh, fine," Carlotta said, fluttering a ringed hand in the air.

The dancers were starting to whisper, the tenor pointedly looking at his wrist even though he couldn't possibly be wearing a watch. His costume, Claire noted, contained zero feathers.

"What's the delay?" Andre asked.

A beat. "No one wants to activate the AI," someone called from the catwalk.

"Whyever not?" Andre called back.

"The core needed to be placed in the center of the hall to measure the full acoustics," the tech called back. He paused. Coughed. "It's in the haunted wing of the catwalk."

One of the dancers giggled. Another one hushed her.

"Oh, for heaven's sake," Carlotta said. "Can we get on with this, please?"

Andre stood and stalked up the center aisle, his usual placid expression replaced with pinched irritation. Apparently no one had informed him that his prized robot-critic wasn't being used. If anything, however, his donors looked intrigued. Several of them—including the grandmother— were studying the catwalk beside the chandelier, as if to catch a glimpse of the Opera Ghost himself.

Maybe Andre was wrong about progressive technology. Maybe all it took to capture patrons was a good old fashioned haunting.

You're welcome, Claire thought.

There was a clatter of ladders, punctuated by Firmin's outraged mutters and the giggles of the dancers. Then, from the rafters, the opera director called, "No ghosts here, I'm afraid. Just an MPAT looking to help. That's 'Music and Performance Assessment Tool,' for the uninitiated."

The donors had looked more impressed by the idea of a ghost.

"I thought it wasn't activated," Carlotta said.

"Sleep mode, probably," Claire replied. "Or it can use exterior cameras to review everything that went on while it was off."

If Carlotta thought Claire's knowledge of AIs was out of the ordinary, she didn't comment. She just shrugged, the corners of her mouth tipping downward. Clearly Claire was not the only person who had places to be tonight. Was Iz gathering the right supplies? Dark clothing, compact tools, soft shoes? Were Astra and Henry noting the right details as they toured the Palais to familiarize themselves with the grounds? They couldn't feel the tech-induced headaches that pounded at Claire's skull whenever she visited. They weren't even convinced the pain she described had anything to do with the AI vault, but Claire knew better. The moment Iz named the Palais, she knew. If she followed the headaches, she'd find the vault.

Claire smoothed the fabric of her dress, impatient. She focused on the theater, forcing her gaze to join everyone else's as they watched Andre navigate the catwalk. It was strange to watch his silhouette moving around Claire's haunting spot. He looked comfortable up there, and she wondered if he'd ever worked as a technician.

"Good evening," the AI said suddenly, its voice stiff and formal like a stuffy old gentleman's. Claire wasn't sorry that it was so different from SATIS's alto tones, though it would be difficult to take the thing seriously.

She wondered if Andre had chosen the voice.

"Tonight's performance was quite good," the AI said.

"Good?!" Firmin huffed. "It was extraordinary!"

"Dancer Meg Giry entered from the wrong wing at the start of Act Two," the AI informed him. "The sopranos in the chorus were 3.4% flat. And Angelique D'Aae, while perfectly pitched, spent half the performance with her crown tipped at an angle."

Claire laughed and adjusted the feathers for the millionth time. "Do you mean the sopranos' notes were 3.4% flat, or they spent 3.4% of the opera flat?"

"The latter," the AI said.

Claire leaned toward Carlotta to make a crack about audience members carrying tuners in their pockets, but the other woman was gathering up her skirts in angry jerks. "Persnickety thing," she said. "No sense of artistry."

And with that, she swept off the stage.

EVENING WAS WELL underway by the time the MPAT finished giving notes. Claire removed her crown as soon as Firmin dismissed them for the night, hurrying backstage ahead of the chorus and narrowly avoiding a chatty baritone. The wings were a flurry of tutus and giggles as costumes were discarded and evening plans were arranged.

Tomorrow was Gala Night. Tomorrow, there would be performances and masks, parades and celebration. Tomorrow, the entire Toccata System would have its eyes on Landry City, and those who could not attend in person would watch jealously from behind the feeds and hope, wish, to travel here one day.

Tomorrow was a perfect opportunity for the Green Cyborg to cause a disaster, and Claire intended to prevent it. Which meant she needed to get moving.

Still, when Claire passed Carlotta's door, she paused. Her understudy had been so agitated this evening. Claire could hear Carlotta moving about inside, shuffling and banging.

Claire hesitated, then lifted a hand to knock on Carlotta's door. It didn't seem right to leave her in distress.

Five more minutes wouldn't hurt anything.

"All right," Carlotta replied. Claire decided to take it as an invitation to enter.

Carlotta had shed her costume for black leggings and a black sweatshirt. Claire didn't know the other singer overly well, but in all their times rehearsing, performing, and enduring donor events together, she'd never seen the woman wearing fewer than three gem-toned colors.

Black was not Carlotta's style.

"Are you planning to haunt the lighting techs in that?" Claire asked.

Carlotta didn't answer. She smoothed her blond curls back over her ears and began wrangling them into a hairband.

"I came to check on you," Claire said.

Even to her own ears, she didn't sound like herself.

She sounded like Iz.

Hair contained, at least for the moment, Carlotta sat on her dressing table bench and tugged midnight blue ballet flats onto her feet. "Where do you think the Phantom Angel hangs around, on a night like tonight?"

Claire blinked, tamping the panic that surged into her chest. But Carlotta had shown interest in the Phantom before, just like most of the people in Landry City. There was no reason for her to suspect Claire.

"I don't know," Claire said slowly. "Why would you need to know that?"

Carlotta stood. "I need their help. It's my nephew. He's missing, and I think he's in trouble."

16

CLAIRE

The Palais reigned dark and silent over its corner of Landry City, lit only by the dancing satellites above.

As soon as Claire vaulted the fence at the back of the grounds, the headache returned. No matter how prepared she was, the sudden throb always set her off balance. It was no more than an annoyance, but it was disconcerting how abruptly it began. Like a flipped switch.

Claire shook it off and surveyed the palace grounds while Astra helped Iz and Henry over the fence that separated the garden from a patch of brambly woodland. The statues were full-on creepy in the dark; the girl peering through the hedge might have been a ghost, and a ring held aloft in a fountain-wizard's palm gave off a sinister glint.

Strange stories. Strange garden.

Claire dialed up her hearing, though it made her cringe to think of sounds bouncing into her throbbing head at extra volume. But there was only the hushing fall of water into the fountains, the stirring of leaves in the trees.

Iz dropped over the fence at her back, her feet hitting the gravel path with an exaggerated scuff.

"Now what?" Astra said.

Claire swallowed, more nervous than she wanted to show. She wasn't used to being at a physical disadvantage. She lowered her hearing back to slightly above normal. "We follow the headache."

Iz's brow pinched in sympathy. Claire tossed her a smile that she meant to look cheerful—or at least casual—but Iz gave her head a little shake, clearly not buying the act.

Five years, and the woman still had her number. It was impressive. And not annoying at all.

As if that wasn't enough, Iz's kindness was wearing off on Claire, too. She had almost agreed to set up a meeting between Carlotta and the Phantom Angel this evening.

Almost. In the end, Claire decided she couldn't delay her search for the AI hearts to help Carlotta. Once she'd saved the city from the Green Cyborg's friends, she could find the missing nephew.

Still, it was hard not to picture Carlotta roaming the streets of Landry City, hoping to run into the Angel. Despite the constant discussion over the city's vigilante, Claire hadn't spent much time considering how the people might view her as a hero, or come to rely on her. It was a strange thought.

She set her guilt aside to focus on the Palais, and the task at hand.

Following a headache to its source was not as complicated as she'd initially thought it might be. She'd pictured the entrance to this heart-vault hidden beneath one of the garden statues, imagined herself playing the world's worst version of hot-or-cold trying to figure out where to search for an entrance.

But as soon as Claire started toward the palace, the pain intensified. Every step made it just a bit sharper.

Pain-or-no-pain. A fantastic party game.

Claire led the others straight up the center of the garden and up to the wall of ballroom doors. They were designed to open straight into the garden so parties could spill onto the paths.

Now, the room was dark. She chose a door and picked the lock with the tool in her ring finger.

"Not a very hard puzzle so far," Astra said.

Claire had to agree. If a headache was all she had to contend with here, the odds of their getting in and out ahead of the Green Cyborg were pretty darn good.

"I'd withhold judgment on that," Henry said.

Astra just shrugged. Claire pushed the door open, and they stepped inside.

As soon as she passed the threshold, the pain in her temple kicked up another notch. She winced, lifting a hand to her head.

Iz set a hand on her arm. "Maybe they have anti-cyborg protections after all. Are you OK to go on?"

Claire gritted her teeth, fighting the urge to lean into Iz's touch. "Yeah. I'm good."

She sensed Iz's objection, but what was she supposed to say? The pain was part of the plan, and so far it was working. So she clenched her jaw and started scanning the walls for anomalies, searching for a secret passage.

The empty ballroom only increased the eerie feeling of the Palais after dark. The wood panels along the wall were lined in strips of gold that caught the gleam of the satellites outside and set the place whirling every time she took a step. Like an escort of fireflies.

It made it tough to concentrate.

About halfway through the room, three panels to the left of dead center, Claire located a latch. It was no more than a pin-sized sliver, but when she flipped it, the panel turned.

Just like the mirror she'd built in her dressing room.

"Impressive," Astra said. "If all it takes to find the hearts is a cyborg on our side, we'll be in and out in fifteen minutes."

There had to be more to it than that. Otherwise, the Green Cyborg wouldn't have dragged his feet in raiding the place. He could no doubt find secret entrances just as easily as she could.

The passage on the other side of the wall felt like the one below the stage at the opera house. A tight corridor that might have been a servants' hall at one time. The others wedged themselves in behind her, shuffling down the passage in single file, and the panel swung shut—taking with it the last remnants of light.

Claire's night vision clicked on, wreathing the passage in green. The pain behind her eyes throbbed in protest, while her sensors alerted her of a high concentration of dust in the air, the smell of wood.

"How are we supposed to see where to go?" Astra said.

"Not so easy now," Henry murmured.

Claire half expected Astra to smack him. Maybe it was good they couldn't see each other.

"I'll guide," Claire said. Her own passage beneath the opera house was lined with lead tiles, the openings made with concealed spring latches rather than anything that would point to an anomaly in the layout. It had taken her months to complete. Here, her scanners immediately picked up a hollow panel in the wall a few paces ahead and to the right.

The caution she'd used in protecting her own home had clearly been worth the effort.

Claire found Iz's hand and held on firmly, hoping the touch felt more businesslike and practical than her hammering heart wanted to admit.

Trapped in a labyrinth and distracted like a teenager. Great. "Everyone hold hands," she said. "If we get separated, we might not find each other again."

Claire set her system to record and map their progress. If this place was really a labyrinth, the difficult part was still ahead.

Beyond the door that left the servants' passage, the walls squeezed even closer. This section felt new. The wood didn't creak so much beneath their feet. Claire paused to scan ahead, and Iz walked into her.

"Sorry," Iz said.

Claire was only glad that Iz couldn't see her blush.

"Maybe you should let us know when you're planning to stop," Astra said.

"Maybe you should walk slowly and be prepared," Claire replied.

"So glad we're all getting along," Henry said.

The next turn wasn't far.

The turn after that led to a closed-off wall. A dead end.

It really was a labyrinth. A human without the ability to scan for anomalies or see through walls—not to mention the dark—could be lost forever. It was a study in patience simply to let Henry lead the way for a few minutes as they backtracked to the previous corridor; there was no room for Claire to squeeze to the front, and therefore no choice.

They continued on, the maze leading them forward in a series of tight coils while her computer system mapped, which at least prevented them from walking in circles or repeating mistakes. Judging by the ever-growing headache at Claire's temples, they were heading in the right direction.

"Maybe they built it this way so thieves would have to be truly dedicated to reach the center," Iz said. "Most people would head home for a cup of tea by now."

Claire grinned into the darkness. Trust Iz to find the humor in any situation. That had always been true.

Three wrong turns later, she opened a door that sent a pulse of feedback screaming through her brain. Claire nearly dropped to her knees. She squeezed Iz's hand, steadying herself against the wall.

"Stop," Astra said, and Claire wanted to scream *No shit* as she clutched her ears, though the sound was coming from inside her head.

It was Iz who maneuvered Claire back through the doorway, where the headache receded to its previous level of annoying-but-probably-not-deadly.

"There's a laser running across the floor," Astra said. "I don't know what it does."

"An alarm, I think," Claire said from outside the door. "I'm getting feedback."

Iz gripped her hand tighter, like she understood what that meant. Maybe so, though the others clearly didn't hear what Claire could. If this was where they stored the hoverrail heart, it would be pretty effective for keeping out cyborgs. At least some of them.

"Looks like a tripwire," Astra said. "We can step over it and we should be fine."

"Should?" Henry asked.

Astra shrugged. Before anyone could speak, she stepped over the light.

Nothing happened.

"If that tripped a silent alarm, we're kind of screwed," Henry said, but he followed her over the laser.

"We have to keep going, anyway," Claire said, nodding to Iz.

Iz let go of her hand and stepped carefully over the laser line.

Claire took a deep breath and plunged back into the room.

The sound came at her from all sides, like someone screaming incessantly inside her mind, like a train trying to roar through her brain with its whistle running nonstop. She tried to focus, but the room turned to water around her.

Iz's hand reached back over the line, steadying.

Claire focused on the light. She moved her right foot over it, and then her left.

The screaming feedback stopped, and Claire allowed herself a beat to exhale.

She felt the difference beneath her feet when they stepped through a new corridor and onto a hollow floor. Even Iz sucked in a breath at the change.

She wasn't surprised, then, when the next door opened straight into a downward-leading staircase. Claire called back a word of warning over her shoulder before descending.

She ran her free hand along the wall as they went down, down. Wood panels turned to stone.

Claire stepped onto the landing.

"Is this the vault?" Henry asked.

"Not yet," Claire said.

But it might be the entrance to the vault. The stairs let out into a circular hall, with faded mosaic tiles on the floor and reliefs carved along the walls. Claire's mapping system informed her they were standing directly below the Palais chapel.

Catacombs. That was...cheerful. There was even an organ against the wall, with shining pipes reaching elegantly for the ceiling. Claire would have expected them to be rusted out, especially if they used this space for an AI safe-zone instead of kingly funerals. Amid piles of dust and cobwebs, the pipes gleamed.

The door at the center of the entrance hall—the only exit aside from the stairs behind them—was shut and locked. It had no keyhole, no latch, not even a sliver of space between the door and the wall. Claire ran her hand along the seam, trying to think over the crashing of the headache that pulsed between her temples like waves breaking on a beach.

It was Astra who pointed to the organ in the wall beside it. "I think it's a code."

Claire followed her gaze, letting the organ crystalize into focus. Yes. Yes, she had to be right. Play the correct tune, and the door would unlock.

Claire approached the organ. She could see clusters of fingerprints on a handful of the keys, all in the middle range of the organ.

Claire arranged the notes in her head, smiling.

Of course.

She touched a thumb to middle C, hesitated, then played the first line of Landry City's anthem.

A beat of silence as the last note faded into the cavelike corridor.

And then, with the grating sound of stone-on-stone, the vault doors opened.

17

CLAIRE

T he ceilings of the chamber were low, the floor made of stone. The room was three times as large as the entrance with the organ, and Claire could picture the ornate Palais chapel ceiling sweeping directly above them. Perhaps this room had been intended to hold centuries of deceased kings and queens, back when they thought royalty would be sticking around on Landry.

No sarcophagi, thankfully, though the solemn carvings along the walls were almost as bad. One angel had her hands clasped at her stony ribcage, her nostrils blackened by a long-lost candle.

Claire's sensors likened the smell of the room to a cave. Damp rock, with undercurrents of soil and stale fire. Everything was old and crumbling.

Everything except the pattern in the floor.

Copper plates dotted the room like dropped coins, each slightly larger than her palm. Claire beelined for the closest one, bending to dig her metal fingertips into the half-inch gap that separated the tile from the stone.

It didn't budge.

Iz dropped to a crouch, her arm brushing against Claire's, and Claire tensed. It was getting harder and harder to focus with Iz at her side, looking beautiful, touching her accidentally. "I bet the hearts are in there," Iz said.

Right. Hidden treasure boxes. There must be a way to make them rise. Another tune? A remote control? Claire scanned the room, dialing back her sensors to block out the scent of Iz's coconut shampoo. She must have showered in one of the travel modules at the port while Claire was in rehearsal.

"Anyone else disconcerted that there's a palace sitting on top of us right now?" Astra said.

Claire ran a finger along the tile again. No button, latch, or keyboard. No hints.

A loud click resounded through the cavern, and the tile shuddered.

Claire leapt back, pulling Iz with her as a stone pedestal pushed the plate out of the floor with an ear-rasping scrape.

All around the room, dozens of columns followed, the scraping so unbearably loud that she longed to cover her ears.

Each pedestal contained a cylindrical glass case, topped by a shining round tile.

Each pedestal held one of Landry City's AI hearts.

"I think that will do the trick."

Claire turned.

The man who had murdered her parents stood silhouetted in the doorway, dwarfing the frame as he ducked to step inside. His feet were shaped into blade-like points, his mask blazing with emerald fury that didn't match his tone.

His tone was triumphant.

Claire scrambled to her feet, moving her body between Iz and the Green Cyborg.

"I have to thank you," he said as the spiky-haired Henchman filed in behind him. The dude looked terrified, shoulders hunched forward like he hoped to shrink into a pile of please-don't-attack-me. "I tried for hours to arrange those smudged keys into the right tune. I'm not so musical, myself." He chuckled. "The Landry City Anthem. How quaint."

Astra was already moving toward him, but the Green Cyborg didn't look concerned. His attention appeared to be fully focused on Claire, but then who could tell? He might have a camera installed in his butt cheek for all she knew.

"Get the hover-rail heart," Claire said quietly to Iz. "And then run."

"I think I should get all the hearts," Iz said.

"Fine. Just go."

Iz scurried away.

To Claire's surprise, Henry followed Iz's lead, diving toward the nearest pedestal and slamming a fist into the glass to scoop up one of the chips. It was a good move; there were a lot of hearts. Any one of them might cause a whole bunch of destruction.

Claire and Astra were the fighters.

Claire launched herself at the Green Cyborg, sending a command to her computer at the same time to draw her knives. The first slid out of her left forearm and into her palm, a comforting weight. She arched toward the Cyborg's neck. It was a guess; his armor didn't give many hints as to where a weapon would meet flesh. He grabbed her arm in defense, and for a moment their strength was matched.

"You're strong," he said, trying to twist her arm around to gain control. "You might consider joining me."

Claire didn't waste energy on an answer. She released the lock between her wrist and her hand, leaving only a wire holding them together. The Green Cyborg lost his grip, and she punched her knife toward his neck again, her hand snapping back to her wrist with a click. He dodged, simultaneously swinging a metal fist at Astra as she attacked from the other side. She ducked and caught hold of his arm, using the momentum to swing onto his back.

The Green Cyborg laughed, plucking her away like an insect.

He tossed Astra into the wall, where she hit the stone with a crack that Claire hoped was not the sound of her spine snapping. She didn't dare look around for Iz, even with her auxiliary camera. She couldn't afford to get distracted.

"See to her," the Green Cyborg said, and it was a testament to how hard Astra had landed that the spiky-haired Henchman made it to her at all. She staggered to her feet, but the Henchman found an ounce of courage and managed to restrain her against the wall.

"Kill her," the Green Cyborg said.

Henry shouted something from across the hall, and Claire heard him running. He was way too far to stop it, to do anything.

Claire wasn't. She abandoned her attack on the Green Cyborg and hurtled toward Astra.

She was halfway there before it registered that the Henchman was just staring at the Green Cyborg, a lost expression on his face.

He wasn't going to kill her. Of course he wasn't.

The Green Cyborg knew it, too. As soon as Claire leapt away from him, he pulled something out of his pocket. The silver box Keyes had given him. Up close, it looked like something that might hold fancy cufflinks.

"Claire," Astra called, her voice thick. "The box. Get the box away from him."

But Claire was already moving to disable the Green Cyborg, cursing herself for her mistake. Iz had said the box was a jammer, but they weren't relying on any AIs for this fight. She wasn't going to get distracted again. She just needed to sink her knife into some flesh.

Claire dove, using her computer system to target.

The Green Cyborg sidestepped, inhumanly fast—or extra-humanly, maybe—and Claire missed, ripping the glove on her right hand to ribbons as she skidded across the stone floor.

One moment, her system was analyzing the footsteps—Henry and Iz tearing back across the room—and the proximity of law enforcement vehicles, which had been alerted to the breach via silent alarm. The next moment, her computer went dark. No network access, no downloaded data on exits and locations. No enhanced hearing. Her sensory analysis of the room vanished, along with the sight in her left eye.

The Green Cyborg had jammed her system. For a moment she could only lie stunned, disoriented.

And then she tried to move.

Her limbs were locked to the floor, as if someone had installed heavy duty magnets in the stone. She might as well have been an ant trapped in a honey jar, an upended roach. All the flailing in the world wouldn't save her.

How long would this last? She nearly called up a systems analysis to check for damage to her circulatory and digestive systems—both of which were aided by the cybernetic enhancements—before realizing that her system analysis would be down, too. She'd grown too used to having superpowers. How long would it take for her blood to start pooling in her limbs?

Fighting a surge of panic, Claire focused on rotating her head.

Her cheek left the floor. It was a small victory, but still. A victory.

Until she saw the Green Cyborg.

He was using Iz as a shield—not that Claire, Astra, or Henry were in any shape to fight him—and he held a knife to her throat. His eyes had gone black; whatever had shut down Claire's computer had stopped his, too.

But he could still move. How?

"Game over," he said. "I have to say, I'm disappointed. I'd thought you to be more resourceful than that."

Claire struggled to get up, to do something. If she could move her head, she could move her limbs. Her body failed to respond. "Gloating," she said through clenched teeth, "how cliché."

"Your love story certainly is. You protect her. Don't deny it."

Iz's eyes were wide, like she wanted tell Claire not to listen, but Claire had no intention of letting him hurt Iz. Ever.

Astra spit a wad of bloody phlegm on the floor, and the Henchman actually flinched. Where had they found this guy? The Discount Thug Warehouse? "Keyes handed off his AI jammer, eh?" Astra said.

And it worked on cyborgs too. Iz had told her the son who designed it wasn't evil, but Claire had her doubts.

"Stay clear of my plans," the Green Cyborg said. "If you do that, your girlfriend will be just fine. Interfere, and she dies."

"You should kill me," Claire said.

"I won't hurt another cyborg, however misguided you might be. I won't be like them. But thank you for making my task that much easier." He plucked the hover-rail heart out of Iz's hands, the motion slow and jerky. Maybe he didn't want to kill Claire because she was a cyborg. Or maybe the jammer was taking a toll on his system, too.

The Green Cyborg pulled Iz out of the room. The Henchman followed, still cringing.

Claire lay in the middle of the floor, helpless. It was like being trapped in that pod all over again, watching as her mother was marched away. Watching as the transport exploded into fire and shrapnel.

She had no way to get to Iz.

If she'd listened to Astra and focused on the jammer, they'd have won.

As the thought passed through her mind, sight returned to her left eye. Her system began to reboot. Either the jammer had a range, or the Green Cyborg had deactivated it. Slowly, she forced herself to her feet.

It was too late. She wasn't fast enough to catch him. She stood in the middle of the cavernous space, utterly alone.

She'd been alone for years. And she'd been fine. Now, Iz was in danger, and Claire had no one to blame but herself. She felt exposed. Unraveled.

A hand squeezed her shoulder, and Claire jumped. Astra stood at her side, eyes glued on the spot where Iz had disappeared. Henry was replacing the rest of the hearts in their pedestals, casting glances toward the ceiling—and the sirens—as he went.

"We'll get her back," Astra said softly.

Claire deserved lectures and anger. Blame. But the rage in Astra's eyes was directed through the arched stone door. At Claire's enemy.

Maybe Claire wasn't alone, after all. It was a strange thought, one she didn't trust. But Astra cared about Iz, too. And they *were* sisters. In a way.

Arm in arm, they helped each other back through the labyrinth. She couldn't help feeling the weight of the angels' judgment, beaming toward her as she left them behind.

18

SAM

Sam's life was a complete and total disaster.

He was supposed to be an errand boy, not a punching bag. Or worse, the guy trying to land a hit *to* a punching bag that just happened to have gone rabid.

He didn't want to punch. He didn't want to *be* punched.

The Cyborg hadn't uttered a word to him since they escaped the Palais. He still wore his mask, and seemed excited to have kidnapped the cyborg woman's girlfriend, who was slung unconscious over his shoulder. Sam kept leaning over to check that she was breathing.

She was.

Sam hated his boss' mask, all those map-like lines etched into the emerald face plate, the angry slits for eyes. He might have been thinking anything.

The Cyborg brought the woman to a warehouse that smelled like coffee and dumped her into a room in the back corner of the third floor. There were no empty warehouses in Landry City—real estate was too pricey for that. Sam wondered whether they were trespassing again, or if this was some kind of a clue as to The Cyborg's identity.

After the girl was secure—and Sam had checked her breathing one more time—The Cyborg turned his angry eyes to Sam.

The Cyborg's eyes were always angry, he reminded himself. No need to jump to conclusions.

"You failed to eliminate her accomplice," The Cyborg said.

Sam opened his mouth. He wanted to say he didn't think it was necessary to kill her, or anyone, that he hadn't taken this job to witness murders—or commit them.

Only a squeak came out.

The Cyborg didn't move. "Your loyalty is in question."

Hell yes, his loyalty was in question. Unfortunately, Sam didn't think the guy would simply allow him to tender his resignation.

Aunt C had been right about this, after all. He should've listened.

"Guard the girl," the Cyborg said. "I'm sending backup in an hour. If she's gone, you will be, too. Understood?"

Sam didn't think it was necessary to answer. He slumped back against the door as the Cyborg glided away. It was eerie, to see someone so large move so silently. It made no sense.

Sam propped his head in his hands. If he stayed, The Cyborg would probably kill him for what had happened at the palace. Still, no matter how he angled the situation, he couldn't picture himself taking action.

Stay and maybe be killed.

Run and definitely be killed.

Nope. He definitely had *not* thought this job through.

19

ISABELLE

Iz woke to the smell of mildew and coffee.

The strange combination made her sit up, confused. Wherever she was, it was dark. A mattress creaked beneath her weight as she moved. She set her feet on the floor and rubbed her face, letting her eyes adjust to the darkness. She could hear someone walking around outside—pacing, even?—but no voices, no music, no traffic to indicate where the room might be located.

Iz stood, testing her balance. She was fine. No injuries. She rubbed her eyes, trying to clear the fuzz from her brain. What would Dad say, if he knew she'd gotten into the middle of yet another battle?

He'd probably say she was just like him. Finding trouble everywhere.

Dad would never be disappointed in her, even if Iz's part in all this had been reduced to 'hostage.' Dad was a hero. Claire was a hero. Even Astra was a hero, when it came down to it.

Iz was just...Iz.

Their mission to the Palais had gone wrong, and Claire's

enemy had swept her away. She wasn't injured. She had no doubt that Claire and Astra would find a way to save the city and help her, too.

In the meantime, Iz would have to do what she could to help herself. She might not be a hero-type, but surely she could start by getting a look at the Green Cyborg.

Iz crossed the small room and knocked on the door. The pacing stopped.

"Excuse me," she said, "may I have a glass of water?"

A pause. Iz doubted the person on the other side of the door was the Green Cyborg, or that such a man would hesitate in the face of the question.

"I doubt your boss wants me to die of thirst before his big plan," Iz said.

Another pause. Then, "Go sit on the bed."

Iz supposed her guard couldn't be faulted for thinking she might fight as well as Claire or Astra.

She sat.

The door opened, revealing the spiky-haired henchman. He was younger than she'd thought, almost fragile looking. He glanced around the room, like he expected her to be hiding an army.

When he seemed satisfied that she was alone, he crossed the room quickly and held out a glass of water. Iz took it, and he turned to go.

"Wait," she said. He stopped. "You saved Astra."

The henchman stopped again. His shoulders sagged. "The boss isn't happy about that."

If the boss were in the building, he wouldn't have said that. Iz must have picked up a tip or two from Astra about reading people.

"Why are you working for him?" Iz asked. It wasn't difficult to keep her tone even. Caring. She actually did want to know. Why would someone like this—timid, clearly not out for a fight—want to work for a terrorist? A monster?

The henchman's shoulders heaved gently. It might have been a laugh, or a sob. When he turned to look at her, his eyes were dry. "Money."

Iz nodded. "Times are hard."

He breathed out, like he'd feared her judgment. Interesting.

"I think," Iz said slowly, "that you might be in over your head."

The henchman stared at her, eyes wide. She met his gaze calmly, sipped the water.

The henchman ran a hand through his hair, which popped right back into its row of mini spikes. He took a breath. Glanced back at the door.

And then, the most miraculous thing happened. He straightened his back. He took a deep breath. And he looked Iz straight in the eye.

"What do you think I should do?"

20

CLAIRE

laire sat in the pilot's seat of the too-small pod, asserting every ounce of her will not to leap up and start pacing across the tiny space. She'd only make herself dizzy. Her head was still swimming after the fight at the Palais, the pain hanging on at the edges. It made her feel blurry. Vulnerable.

What was the Green Cyborg doing with Iz? He said he'd keep her safe, as insurance, but how could Claire trust that? Maybe he'd kill Iz to get her out of the way. Maybe he'd drug her, take her off Landry, hide her in an underground cell forever.

The longer Claire thought about it, the more dire the situation seemed. Her thoughts whipped and tangled, and she wanted to spring out of the chair, claw at the ceiling, tear through the city. She forced herself to stay, to breathe. If she wanted to help Iz, she needed to recover.

Henry was patching up a cut on Astra's arm, the two of them trading glances as if they could communicate through their thoughts. Maybe they could. Claire wanted to ask

Henry how he could even see the damn bandage through those googly eyes.

Claire missed Iz.

"We have to save her," Claire said. "It's not even a question."

Astra and Henry exchanged another meaningful look. They didn't even say anything, didn't argue, but in an instant Claire's anxiety shifted to red-hot anger.

"I chose Landry City over your SATIS girls, and Iz got kidnapped because of it," she said. She heard how defensive she sounded. She didn't care. "Every time I choose Landry City, bad shit goes down. If I'd left the heart alone, the Green Cyborg wouldn't have it."

Now the city was in danger, because of Claire. Iz, too.

"He'd have found a way," Henry said gently.

"But I showed it to him," Claire said. "I opened the door."

She'd handed him every AI heart in the city, practically on a silver platter, because she didn't trust anyone else to protect the things she loved.

It was her fault.

"Yeah, you did," Astra said. Henry finished wrapping her hand, and she gave him a pat that felt far too loving in contrast with the rest of her before turning to face Claire. "We all had a hand in that, Ms. Phantom Angel. In case you've forgotten, we made the plan together."

Claire had convinced them. Claire had led the way.

"We need to save Iz *and* stop this guy's plan for Landry," Astra said.

Claire gaped at her would-be sister. What the hell kind of pie-in-the-sky idea was that? "We don't know where she is, or anything about his plan. How are we supposed to do that?"

Every time she crossed the Green Cyborg, she lost. Every time she chose Landry City—over SATIS, over trusting her parents, over Iz when they were kids—she lost.

"I spent a few more years with SATIS than you did," Astra said. "I've got some skills."

Claire refrained from snapping that she had skills, too. Her skills had gotten them through the maze and into the vault.

Little good that it did any of them. Her skills weren't the problem.

The console behind Claire beeped, and she nearly jumped through the ceiling. Which could have been extremely bad for the ship, given she could literally punch through the roof without thinking about it.

Henry leaned over her and pressed some buttons. "Visitor outside the doors."

"Video?" Astra said.

Henry pushed more buttons, and the spiky-haired Henchman's face blinked up at them from the screen.

"I'm going to kill him," Claire said. "Be right back."

"No," the Henchman said. "Iz sent me. Please let me in. Before he realizes I'm gone."

Claire looked at Astra, who shook her head. "Fifty-fifty it's a trap."

"Iz wouldn't give up our location," Henry said.

Claire didn't think she would, either. Besides, the Green Cyborg hadn't been all that interested in chasing after them. If he'd wanted to kill them, he could have done it back in the vault.

"Please," the Henchman said.

It could be a trap. Was probably a trap. But the Henchman would know where the Green Cyborg was keeping Iz.

"Let's escort him inside," Claire said.

It was all she could do to keep from punching the Henchman in the face when they did. He stood in the center of the floor, hands open at his sides, eyes trained on his shoes.

Henry watched the screen for more visitors. Astra guarded the door.

Claire stayed in her seat, arms crossed, and waited for him to talk.

"He's going to blow up the main hover-rail station," the Henchman said.

"Why would you tell us that?" Astra asked. "Out of the goodness of your heart?"

"Look," the guy said, practically wringing his hands, "I took this job to pay the bills. To get ahead. I was supposed to be an errand boy. Not a killer. I love Landry City, too. I don't want people to die."

Claire laughed, bitter. "A bit late."

The Henchman actually winced. "Yeah, I know. But Iz said if I came and helped you—"

"Where is she?" Claire interrupted. She wasn't interested in whatever promise of redemption Iz might have offered this kid.

"They're moving her," he said. "That's how I got away. The Cyborg, he compartmentalizes. We know what we need to know, as we need to know it."

Disappointment bloomed across Claire's chest, painful. "Why didn't you bring her?"

The Henchman's face crumpled, and Claire almost believed he was worried about Iz, too. Almost. "She said I shouldn't. She said her absence would tip him off to my betrayal and to tell you to save the city. She trusts you, and she has it handled."

Astra huffed out a breath of annoyance. "She's probably baking him cookies and listening to his life story right now."

"Kindness isn't the same as weakness," Henry said softly.

Claire fell somewhere in the middle. Yeah, Iz gave people the benefit of the doubt, far more than Claire ever did. That had always been true. But she was also resourceful and savvy.

If Iz trusted Sam, then Claire would try to trust him, too. She kept her attention on the Henchman. "OK, so you don't know where they're moving her. But you know about the hover-rail station?"

The Henchman nodded. "I get the feeling there's more to it, though. Like I said, he—"

"Compartmentalizes," Astra said. "Let me guess. He's going to frame the hover-rail AI for the job."

"Yeah," the Henchman said. "Yeah, but AI framing is always in the mix.... He works for that big-wig—"

"Keyes," Henry provided, still watching the screen.

"Sure, Keyes. He's got it out for AIs. I don't know why. But The Cyborg's got his own agenda."

Claire clenched her hands in her lap. This pod of theirs already felt too small, but at the moment it was positively stifling. "I suppose it's too much to hope that you know his name."

The Henchman frowned. "I've been calling him 'The Cyborg,' haven't I? I have no idea."

Astra laughed, but Claire couldn't see what was funny. The other woman seemed to realize it; she shrugged. "I didn't think this one had any sass in him."

"Astra likes to be surprised about people," Henry said. "Doesn't happen much."

"So?" the Henchman said. "You believe me? You'll help?"

Claire looked to Astra, who said, "Far as I can tell, he's not lying."

Henry nodded in agreement.

Or he was really good at lying, and Claire's choice would end with her city destroyed, and the woman she loved...

She couldn't finish the thought.

They needed a lead. This was it. There was as much risk in ignoring the Henchman's intel as there was in taking action. And if anyone could convince a bad guy to turn good, it was Iz.

Claire studied the Henchman. So she'd work with the guy. It didn't mean she had to trust him entirely. "What's your name?" she asked.

His shoulders dropped, and he let out a breath of relief. "Sam."

Claire frowned. No doubt there were multiple Sams in the city. But the age, and the timing... "Don't tell me your aunt works at the opera," she said.

Sam blinked, confused. "Sure. She's a singer."

Carlotta's nephew. Claire sighed. "I guess I can cross finding you for her off my to-do list."

"You know my aunt?"

"Yup."

"Shit."

Astra laughed again. It was disconcerting.

Claire ignored her. If anything, the information made her trust her decision a tiny bit more. "All right. When's this hover-rail situation going down?"

Sam licked his lips. "Tomorrow night. The station will be packed. More people than usual."

"Why?" Astra asked.

But Claire already knew, because she was the main

event. And with Toccata's golden beams already making overtures at the pod's portholes, it wasn't tomorrow anymore: it was today.

"It's the end of opera season," Claire said, dread welling in the pit of her stomach. "It's Gala Night."

21

CLAIRE

Gala Night marked the end of opera season, the last hurrah of the summer. More than any other night in the whirlwind of Landry City's music season, the streets were packed with festival goers and tourists who had saved their pennies—possibly for years— for a once-in-a-lifetime chance to take part in the dizzying carnival.

Claire stood in the center of the hover-rail station, her vigilante persona wrapped in a layer of public-appropriate veiling that made her feel overly stuffed. But the crowd was so thick tonight, the variations in costuming so wild—cat masks and horned headpieces, wings and hooves and claws —that she blended in better than ever. She scanned their faces, trusting her computer to recognize the Green Cyborg's cronies even if she didn't.

She didn't want to have to drain her system by activating her x-ray vision. Not yet.

Most of the people packed into the glass box of the hover-rail station were not headed for the opera house. They might stand in the city square surrounded by rushing fountains, watching musical highlights from projections on the walls of the shining towers. They might stay near the river to watch the procession of glowing boats under the Glass Bridge, a nod to Landry's satellites—many of which were lit up in green and gold as they passed over the city, extending Gala Night into space.

Wherever they were headed, they used the hover-rail to get there.

And Claire couldn't risk evacuating them. Not yet. If she did, the Green Cyborg would know she was taking action. He'd kill Iz.

Astra and Sam patrolled the balcony level, though Claire kept losing them in the chaos. Henry was out of sight, ready to set off alarms and get the crowd to safety as soon as Claire located the bomb.

How they'd get to Iz fast enough, even if they managed to spoil the Green Cyborg's plan...they hadn't figured that part out yet. It made Claire's stomach burn with fear.

"Sam says we've got company. Stairwell B," Astra said, her voice buzzing into Claire's ear. "They have a package."

Claire would have been able to find her way there even without her computer's assistance, just by following Astra's journey through the balcony. She disrupted the flow of the crowd as she ran, causing people to bulge toward the railings with startled looks. Since he wasn't a fighter, Sam would have melted away to help Henry with the evacuation process.

Claire hoped she and Astra could handle whatever fight was waiting for them. She darted across the lobby, allowing the crowd to part for her and ignoring the shouts that chased her across the floor. She flung open the door to the corner stairwell and threw herself up. Footsteps pounded above, punctuated by Astra's shouts.

The Green Cyborg's machine-legs would have been pretty handy right about now.

Astra was half a flight ahead of her when their quarry banged the last door open. The henchie looked back, and Claire recognized the woman whose hair Iz had pulled during the fight at the opera house. She had indeed cut it short. Rather gratifying, really.

One flicker of Claire's x-ray confirmed the package in the woman's hands contained the bomb.

"She's on the roof," Astra said as the woman bounded into the night. "Nowhere to go but down. Henry? Be a dear and work on that evacuation thing, will you?"

Together, they stormed the roof. The woman with the box stepped back as Claire advanced, clutching the package to her chest.

"Don't want me to kick that box while you're still up here, do you?" Claire said.

The woman glanced to the side. It was all the warning Claire had, but it was enough. "She's got an escort," Claire shouted, a split second before a man flew out of his hiding place and straight into Astra. She deflected his blows easily, not even breathing hard.

Claire expected more cronies to pour across the roof, but no one else appeared. The Green Cyborg had only sent two people.

He was still underestimating her. No, he was underestimating *them*.

Claire rushed at the woman with the bomb as Astra flipped her partner onto his back. The henchwoman backed toward the edge of the roof, glancing behind her as if scared she'd fall while holding the bomb. Below, a fire alarm blared.

Claire simply nudged the woman toward the edge of the roof. "What next?"

The woman hesitated.

And then she threw the bomb at Claire.

Claire dove for the box as the woman vaulted back toward the stairs. She caught the package by the edges, the momentum nearly knocking it out of her grip again.

"Nice catch," Astra said. Claire hadn't seen much of her fight, but her opponent's nose gushed blood and his eyes were closed. He was breathing, noisily, but Claire didn't think he was conscious.

Claire hadn't bothered to be afraid of her SATIS sister, even though she knew full well what it meant to have been trained by the AI. She thought perhaps she ought to revise that attitude. Sirens screamed nearby, headed for the supposed fire. Landry City's first responders were nothing if not quick. On Gala Night, they'd probably send the whole fleet.

"How do we disarm it?" Astra asked.

Claire eased the lid of the box open and let her computer tell her what to do. One wire snip. That was all it took. The wrong one would have blown them to bits, but Claire had no trouble trusting her computer.

She didn't want to think about how she would have deactivated the bomb if the Green Cyborg had been here with his jammer. After her failure with Iz, it was impossible to ignore. She'd come up against him again, and soon. She needed to know how to beat him.

With the wires snipped and the bomb dismantled, Claire let the tools in her hand retract and stood. "That was easy," she said. "I don't like easy."

Below them, the streets squirmed, people packed so tightly after evacuating the station that Claire couldn't imagine how they moved at all. Emergency lights flashed, the station's alarm still blaring.

Astra gripped her shoulder. "Let's go find Iz."

Across the city, the Glass Bridge exploded. Claire saw the flash, followed by a shower of glass that sparkled like rising snow. A wave of shouts wove through the city, delayed by distance, and Claire imagined people diving for cover, throwing arms over their heads, shielding children from the raining shards.

Smoke rose to mix with glitter. It was grotesquely beautiful.

Astra's eyes were on the street below the station, where a line of ambulances and police cars had responded to the station's evacuation call. "They can't cross the bridge," she said. "What's on the other side of the bridge?"

Claire looked over her city, the smoke spreading like a malicious fog.

Beyond the river was the crown jewel of Landry City, the cultural symbol of the entire system. "This was a distraction," she said. "He's going to hit the opera house."

PART 4

FINALE

22

CLAIRE

The street was awash in chaos when Claire and Astra left the station. People cried and coughed and pointed at the smoky sky, where the satellites blinked like confetti through the violent haze. Emergency vehicles peeled away toward the bridge. The crowd squeezed and jostled, a blur of color and fear.

A woman vomited by the curb. A man yelled out instructions, but Claire couldn't hear him well enough to tell if he meant to direct traffic or begin a sermon.

She'd saved their lives. It wasn't enough.

The men waited for Claire and Astra in a neighboring alley, Henry with his hands stuffed in his pockets, and Sam smoking a cigarette with trembling fingers.

Claire led them underground.

"You bring us into a lot of dark passages," Astra said as she followed Claire from the maintenance grate and into the network of tunnels that Claire had spent the last year memorizing.

Claire turned a corner, beckoning the others along. "I'm good like that."

"These tunnels go under the river?" Henry asked. He was breathing hard, while Astra jogged along behind Claire without any apparent issue while Sam brought up the rear.

"There used to be cars in the city," Claire said. "A long time ago. They couldn't cross the Glass Bridge, so they used the tunnel. It's closed now."

"Right, great," Henry said. "So it's stable?"

Claire shrugged. Before the explosion, yes. Now? She hoped so. It was the only route. "Sam," she said, "if you know anything else about our cyborg friend, now's the time to share. You said he has his own agenda. You don't know what it is?"

"I know he hates Landry City," Sam said, his voice echoing along the concrete walls. "He's been gathering funds from the rich. I don't know how. He seems to think he's some kind of Robin Hood."

"That'd explain the green," Henry said.

"Who's Robin Hood?" Astra asked.

Claire jumped over a crack in the pavement. "Story time later."

"I just know they did something to him, treated him badly," Sam said. "Someone rich did. Or all of them. I'm not sure, but he's punishing everyone."

Definitely sounded like the Green Cyborg from Transport A90D. Claire could still hear his rambling speech, his protestations of mistreatment. He'd massacred a transport full of innocent employees to get revenge on the company that abused him.

Claire turned them around another corner, hurrying past the remnants of an old archaeological dig. One of the many projects that had been abandoned as Landry City focused on its future.

"Gathering funds," Claire repeated. It tugged her mind toward a connection that made no sense. And yet...she thought of all the fundraising events she'd attended at the opera house, all those people opening their wallets to sit at hightop tables surrounded by champagne and flower arrangements. She thought of the donors who'd attended last night's rehearsal, and the old woman whose granddaughter was such a fan.

I hate dancing for donated coin, but alas it must be done.

Andre. He'd been praised for his visionary changes to the opera, yes. But he'd also been praised—again and again —for ensuring its future. He'd been going after endowments. Wills.

Claire moved faster.

They emerged from the narrow tunnel and into a long wide one, the former route for cars passing beneath the river. Claire had never seen a car that wasn't an emergency vehicle; the hover-rail was more than enough to keep the city moving. A line separated the tunnel through the middle for no apparent reason.

She tried not to think of the river rushing above, or the smoke. Or the collapsing Glass Bridge.

She could only do one thing.

She ran.

The tunnel was blocked at the other end, but Claire already knew this. She found her maintenance hole and scurried inside.

No one sighed at the tightness of the passage.

Onward they ran, until Claire reached the false wall she'd installed herself. She flipped the panel and stepped inside.

"Not another labyrinth," Astra said.

"It is," Claire said. "But this one's mine."

She led them easily through the maze and into the opera house, straight through the mirror to her dressing room.

Where Firmin stood, agitated, in the center of the space. Carlotta sat on the dressing table, legs crossed. Firmin's eyes went as wide as his jaw when Claire entered through the mirror and paused in surprise. Collecting herself quickly, Claire unhooked her mask. There was no point in maintaining the facade, not when revealing her identity would save precious moments.

Carlotta lifted a painted eyebrow. The woman was as unflappable as a rock.

Until she saw Sam. When the ex-henchman crowded inside behind Astra, Carlotta flew off the dressing table and threw her arms around him, simultaneously hugging and hitting him.

Claire held up a hand to stop Astra from taking any action that might end with cleaning blood off the wall.

"You're alive," Carlotta said. "You stupid boy, you're alive."

Claire's dressing room wasn't small, but six people certainly made it seem so. Firmin stared at them all, sputtering, and Claire almost regretted that she'd never hear whatever scathing speech he'd surely been preparing. "You're —you're—"

"Late?" Claire offered.

"The Phantom Angel!"

Why stop there? "And a cyborg," Claire said.

"This is—I can't—"

Carlotta let go of Sam and made her way back to Firmin, wiping tears from her cheeks. She couldn't keep her eyes off her nephew, as if he might vanish again the moment she blinked. Sam's face was bright red.

"I assume there's trouble?" Carlotta said, voice shaking with emotion.

Claire nodded. "We need to get to Andre's office."

Carlotta didn't waste time on confusion. "It should be empty. He's going to do his welcome speech in five minutes."

"Can you delay him?"

Carlotta returned a sly smile. "But of course, my intriguing colleague. In return for the full story of...this."

"If I survive tonight, you've got a deal."

Carlotta looked around Claire to Sam, as if she could drink him in. "You should stay with me."

Claire fully expected the kid to take the excuse and go running to his aunt. Out of the line of fire, and out of Claire's hair. She surprised herself by realizing she didn't really blame him, after all this.

Instead, Sam stood up a little straighter. He squared his shoulders. "I think I should help them. I think... No, I have to. I have to fight."

Carlotta opened her mouth as if to protest, then closed it. "I suppose...yes, I suppose you do. She patted her nephew on the cheek with a tenderness that made a lump rise in Claire's throat.

Carlotta didn't tell him to be careful. She didn't have to.

When she swept out of the room, she dragged a still-sputtering Firmin with her.

"I don't trust that one," Astra said. "He might talk."

It was a definite possibility. But what were they supposed to do, tie him up? His absence would be suspicious, for starters. "Then we'd better hurry," Claire said. "Spread out on the main floor. Be ready to fight, or evacuate the hall."

Astra cracked her knuckles. "How about both?"

"Probably," Claire said. "I'm going to get Iz."

"What if she's not there?" Henry asked.

Claire threw up her hands. How had these people defeated SATIS without her to talk them through it? "Then I'll radio you. I know the opera house better than anyone. And don't go poking around under the floorboards without me."

"Why?" Sam asked. "What's there?"

Claire gave him a grim smile. "You really don't want to know."

23

ISABELLE

I z wished she'd called Dad after all. Not for advice—
even hero-Dad would be out of his depth here, unless
he was hiding secret adventures Iz hadn't heard of. No,
she wished she'd called to say goodbye. Just in case.

The Green Cyborg had peeled off his armored helmet
the moment they reached his office in the opera house,
meticulously disguising the rest of his mechanical body in
what she could only assume was a custom-tailored suit. His
shoes snapped over his knife-blade feet, and he applied a
layer of plastic skin over the metallic curve of his jaw,
humming as he worked.

Andre didn't seem concerned about displaying his secret
identity to Iz. He hadn't even bothered to tie her up. He'd
just plopped her into a puffy, flower-printed chair and
instructed her not to move. The office smelled like metal
and grease, more like a ship's bay than an administrator's
workspace, and Iz thought with a pang of her old racer, the
Bullet Dragon she'd left behind at the Star Leaders Academy. She hoped someone was taking good care of it after all
the chaos on the *Traveler*.

She wondered if she'd ever fly it again.

Display cases full of old props lined Andre's office walls, stuffed with sabers and masks, candlesticks and earrings, and even a pair of elaborately embroidered shoes. A holographic model of the opera house flickered in the center of Andre's desk. To Iz's left, the shelves were packed with antique pistols, sleek black laser guns, and stunners.

It took a moment to realize the weapons weren't props. Iz didn't think Dad had ever needed to use a gun—his heroics were more of the search-and-rescue variety—but he'd carried one as part of the Quadra Moon Guard.

Iz knew the difference between fake guns and real ones.

It was a brilliant hiding place, actually. Firearm access was strictly controlled in the system. Who would think to check that a prop gun was actually a prop?

Andre practically danced around the room, singing under his breath as he pinned golden cufflinks to his sleeves and arranged his hair. If she hadn't known his identity, she might not have noticed the careful spring in each step that kept his feet from falling too heavily on the floorboards, or the nearly inaudible clicks from the mechanisms whirling inside his body.

The handsome opera manager with the silver-dusted hair would never risk showing her his secret identity if he intended to be true to his word. There was no doubt in Iz's mind; he meant to harm her.

"You know," Andre said, speaking so suddenly that Iz jumped, "stealing my Henchman was a low blow."

He was still pinning his cufflink, a small smile on his face. As if he were discussing the price of box seats, or inviting her to spend a day at the races.

"How do you know he didn't leave on his own?" Iz said.

Andre just smiled. "That coward? He wouldn't dare."

"Do you even know his name?"

Andre scoffed. "What would be the point? They're interchangeable, and disposable."

Poor Sam. No wonder he'd jumped ship. "Then you shouldn't mind that he's gone."

Andre plucked a small silver box off of the desk and turned it around in his palm before slipping it into his pocket.

Keyes's jammer. Iz's throat tightened, her chest barely containing painful anger. No wonder Edward Keyes got along with this criminal. He'd treated his own son like a disposable asset.

Conor, who thought with his brain instead of his fists, who designed that jammer to defy his father and died as a consequence, would have done anything to get it out of Edward Keyes's hands.

Conor was dead. But Iz was still here.

She might not be able to kick people's teeth out when they hurt those she loved. She might not be an assassin, an AI expert, or a fighter pilot.

But she was good with people. Not the way Astra was good with people, divining their inner workings with almost supernatural ease. Iz made people feel comfortable. Iz encouraged them to talk.

Oh, she wasn't naive enough to think she could coax Andre into showing mercy. Andre and Sam were entirely different creatures, and she'd merely nudged Sam in a direction he'd already longed for.

But she might be able to get information. She might be able to get the jammer.

"Are you going to set off a bomb?" she asked, adding a little tremble to her voice. It wasn't difficult. Less like acting than opening a valve to a feeling she already held at bay.

"Better." Andre ran a finger along one of the prop displays, as though checking for dust. "You see, the theater has an unfortunate gas leak. And we're going to discover it tonight. I can blow up the chandelier with a thought. When I do, the VIPs of Landry City will give up their ghosts. And their cash."

He chuckled, pleased at his joke. Iz wondered if he'd been saving that one and decided he had.

"Tell me," he said, "do you think your little cyborg friend can breathe poison?"

Iz didn't know how Claire could possibly know to show up here tonight. Sam certainly hadn't been aware of any opera house massacre plans. But Claire was resourceful. So was Astra.

She had to believe in them. And in the meantime, she'd help.

"She'll choose me," Iz said. "We'll escape."

Andre smirked. "Don't be so sure."

He still spoke like he was discussing his ideas for next season's staging of Puccini. So calm.

She needed to get him to come close.

Heart racing, Iz stood. When Andre didn't object, she wandered to the prop case, watching his reflection in the glass as he pinned a rose to his lapel. "You really think she'll choose the city over me?" Iz asked.

"Most certainly."

Iz hooked a finger around the latch of the prop case. She didn't expect to get her hands on a gun; she wanted to see what Andre would do if she tried.

He crossed the room in two wide steps and grabbed her arm, tugging her back toward the chair. The movement would have been casual, unconcerned even, except for the painful pressure of his fingers on her wrist.

Which told her two things. One, that she was correct in her guess about the weapons being real.

Two: they were loaded.

"It was a good thought, darling," he said, "but I don't have time to play. I'll have to ask that you put your hands in your lap so I can secure them. I know how cliché it is, but I can't spare a guard."

Especially since he couldn't trust them. Iz held her hands obediently in front of her body. "Can't blame a girl for trying."

Andre wrapped a thick rope around her wrists, the pockets of his open coat brushing the floor at his feet. "Leave the subterfuge to your vigilante friend," he said.

"OK," Iz said.

And then she slammed her forehead into the crest of bone above his eye.

Andre lurched back in surprise, slapping a hand to his face as the half-knotted rope slipped off of Iz's hands. Head swimming, she dipped her fingers into his pocket, and edged the jammer out, catching it between her feet.

"Sorry," she said, stars still blinking in her vision as she shoved the box beneath the chair's flowered skirt. "I guess that might leave a bruise. How do your opera patrons feel about black eyes?"

Andre ran a finger along the bone as though testing for a fracture. Iz couldn't help thinking that Astra would have been proud of her.

Claire, too.

Maybe Iz could be helpful in a fight, after all.

Andre recovered himself enough to wrench Iz's hands behind her, tying them awkwardly around the thick chair back before bending to bind her ankles. His anger was slow burning, controlled. He wasn't the sort of person to give in to blind rage.

He was the sort of person who kept his calm long enough to plot mass murders.

"My opera patrons will be too dead to notice any bruises," he said. "I'm afraid I'm not sorry to tell you that the gas leak will extend to the administrative offices. This is good-bye, Mademoiselle."

"It's been a pleasure," Iz said.

Andre gave her a short bow and an incongruously warm laugh, still prodding at his forehead. And then he slipped out the door.

Iz couldn't see the jammer sitting behind her feet, but she knew it was there. She only hoped Andre wouldn't notice its absence until it was too late.

She shifted, uncomfortable, but she couldn't help smiling. When Claire showed up to fight the Green Cyborg tonight, she'd be the one with the edge.

And it was Iz who'd made it happen.

24

CLAIRE

C laire was ready to bash through any barrier—skulls included—to get to Iz. Fortunately, though, the journey to the admin floor was relatively obstacle free. Three flights of stairs, a couple dozen startled opera goers, and one easily picked lock, and she was there.

Iz sat restrained in the center of the opera director's overstuffed office, hands wrenched so tightly behind her that her shoulders curved back. Andre was going to pay for that. Majorly.

Iz's eyes widened at the sight of Claire. "You," she said, "were supposed to save Landry City."

Trust Iz to be thinking of everyone else first. Claire would have smiled, if she hadn't been so worried. She knelt and cut the ropes, cursing Andre for every mark they left on Iz's skin as she took Iz's wrist in her hand and rubbed the spot where they'd bitten into her flesh.

"I am saving Landry City," she said. "He's going to blow up the opera house."

Iz shook her head, her curls brushing against her cheeks

as she moved. "No, Claire. He's going to *poison* the opera house."

Claire blinked. "But—the hover-rail station—the bomb—"

"I don't know about that. But he's planted spigots in the chandelier. After he delivers his victory speech, they'll burst and fill the theater with poisonous gas."

Revenge and reward, wrapped up in a neat little package.

Iz's hands were still in hers, and for the first time since their reunion, Claire couldn't think of a reason to pull away. Unless it was to tuck a wayward strand of hair behind Iz's ear, or cup a gentle hand to the back of her neck. Something had brought them together again—whether coincidence or the universe, she didn't know—and Claire had wasted so much time trying to fight it, afraid that Iz would reject her.

From the moment of their reunion, Iz had accepted her as she was, metal parts and all. She'd told herself that their differences were more deeply seated, that it was about a fundamental dissonance between them. Landry City versus adventure in the system. Iz's goodness versus Claire's dysfunction.

Maybe it had been about Claire's fear all along. "The way we left things," she said, "before the transport. The fight. It was my fault."

It was such a long time ago.

Iz lifted her head and kissed Claire so suddenly that Claire gasped in surprise before she realized she ought to return the kiss.

Which she did.

For a moment, she was sixteen again, her girlfriend's perfect lips soft against hers. Iz tasted of mint and lavender. Of home.

Iz deepened the kiss, desperate. If they hadn't been in the middle of a battle, Claire would have locked the door and swept all the junk off Andre's desk. Sex in the enemy's office. Why the hell not?

"We were kids," Iz said, her breath warm against Claire's cheek. "It's in the past. Let's make sure Landry City has a future."

The future. Claire hadn't imagined hers with Iz in it, but now the world felt wide open. Her hope wasn't tied to Landry City; it was knotted to Iz. And maybe with Astra and Henry, too. Maybe it wasn't so dangerous to assemble a family, after all.

"I'm going to deactivate the poison," Claire said. "When I get back to the hall, help Sam get everyone out. The only problem is the jammer."

Which she still didn't know how to get past.

Weirdly, Iz grinned. And then she bent down and reached under the chair, plunging her hand beneath the ugly floral dust curtain.

When she came back up, she was holding a small silver box. The jammer. She set it in Claire's hand. "I thought this might help. Actually, I thought its absence would help, but since you're here you might as well take it."

Claire stared at her. "How—but—"

Iz's smile widened. "I have tricks up my sleeve, too, you know."

Yes. Like turning a Henchman to the good side, and stealing the enemy's most precious weapon. "Those aren't tricks," Claire said. "Those are goddamn superpowers."

Iz wasn't done. She pointed to one of Andre's glass display cases. "Those guns are real, too. You might want to take one."

"You are amazing."

Iz nodded, flushing, and Claire loved her. "How will I know when you're back in the hall?" Iz asked.

Claire kissed her again before pulling reluctantly away. She swiped a laser gun from the shelf—anything bigger would only weigh her down—and slipped the jammer into her pocket. "I'm a diva, darling. I know how to make an entrance."

25

CLAIRE

Tonight, the catwalks were crowded.

Claire did her best to swing from the fixtures, to make her way above the heads of the lighting technicians. The audience was excited, drunk on the glamor of Gala Night, decked in sequins and gold.

They didn't know about the bridge, or the near-disaster at the hover-rail station. They didn't know they were in danger.

How Andre had kept that information from spreading here via messages and news apps, she couldn't guess. He had the jammer. He must have other resources, too.

There would be celebrities here tonight, leaders from throughout the system. Their deaths would be blamed on an AI, or several. For what purpose, Claire didn't know. Keyes's plans were bigger than revenge.

They'd take him on next.

First, she had a massacre to stop.

"What kind of poison is it?" Astra said in her ear as Claire swung from one precarious handhold to another.

"Astra knows poison," Henry said helpfully.

"I don't think the Green Cyborg gave Iz specifics," Claire said.

"You didn't ask?" Astra said.

Claire used a trio of pipes as monkey bars, tucking her feet up to avoid kicking a lighting tech in the back of the head. "Like you would have?"

"She would have," Henry said.

Well. Claire had been preoccupied. She swung over to the abandoned limb beside the chandelier, landing as quietly as she could. "My system can identify the poison. Can you stop it?"

"If we have the right materials on hand, yes."

Great. That was a start. "Let's just hope it doesn't ask for fairy dust."

Claire climbed over the rail of the catwalk and swung her grapple toward the chandelier as the curtain parted below. A brief pause, and Andre stepped out onto the stage to a wave of enthusiastic applause. He looked so small from here.

So...*squishable.*

Had Keyes subsidized the purchase of Andre's eye implants? Or the hand that looked so real it probably needed sunscreen in the summer? She knew how lethal his feet were, yet he didn't even hide them in boots. He wore regular shiny black dress shoes.

No wonder she hadn't realized.

Part of her wanted to shove her hand into her pocket and use the jammer right now, to prevent him from activating the gas. But if she did that, she'd be taking herself out of the fight. Andre might be surprised for a second, but he'd been able to move back in the tombs with his computer stalled.

Besides, Andre seemed like the kind of guy with a

backup plan or two. He wouldn't rely on his system alone to set off the gas in the chandelier.

She had to wait.

While Andre basked in the applause, Claire focused on her route to the chandelier. Right now, all the hurrying stage techs were masking her presence. If she used her grapple to get to the chandelier, she'd swing too low. She'd catch someone's attention—maybe even Andre's.

Claire stowed her grapple. And then she jumped.

The chandelier shuddered under her weight, and Claire crouched at the top, hoping no one had noticed. The fixtures rattled with musical clinks, but the audience was giving Andre a standing ovation simply for stepping onto the stage.

Claire's main concern was that she'd inadvertently released the gas.

Her system wasn't giving her any warnings. A good sign.

When the doors swung shut with a crash that echoed through the hall, the applause stuttered but didn't die. Claire risked a glance at the back of the theater, where heavily armed guards were now stationed at each door.

They wore gas masks.

"You'll forgive me for interrupting your celebration," Andre said, his tone so pleasant that he might have been discussing next season's selections. Mozart or Gluck? Perhaps something contemporary?

"This city." Andre sighed. Shook his head. He was enjoying this. "This city hates me."

The last of the applause petered out, as though the audience wasn't quite sure whether to take the comment as a joke. The gas-masked guards might have been part of the show. A Gala Night demonstration.

Andre, Claire thought, was counting on that.

Claire gripped the chandelier fixture with her robotic hand and began scanning the lights for anomalies. But this was a unique item, not something her computer could compare with similar models or structures. There were no unlit bulbs, nothing to tip her off at a glance.

Claire activated her x-ray vision.

At first, they all looked identical. They were just lights.

And then she caught one with a glass cylinder at the center. Like a deadly little beaker, screwed in beneath the burning filament. Her computer locked onto it, locating nine more.

Jackpot.

"OK," Astra said when Claire described them, "do you have a probe? Something you can use to test them?"

She did, but she'd have to let go of the fixture to use it. Claire steadied herself on the balls of her feet, leaned her weight toward the center of the chandelier. Thank the stars the thing was so massive.

She unscrewed the bulb, her robotic hand immune to its heat, and pierced the top with the slim knife in her pinky finger. Her system ran a stream of information across her digital eye, already identifying the substance as toxic, and processing specifics.

On the stage, Andre held up a hand as though someone had protested his statement about the city hating him. "Hear me out. I've done good things for the opera, wouldn't you agree? Many of you believe so fully in the improvements I've made that you've bequeathed large amounts of money to be donated to the opera upon your deaths."

Claire's system blinked, and she read the results to Astra, who swore. "Right. OK, well, don't expose it to air."

"Assumed that part."

"Your friend Andrew must have wanted an easy way out of this, in case something went wrong," Astra said.

"Andre."

"Whatever. You diffuse the gas by inserting a drop of water. You must have a pipe of water in your body, right? Just poke your pinky in and voila. Diffused."

"I don't have a water pipe in my body. Why would I have a water pipe in my body?"

Astra tsked. "That's inconvenient."

"Does it have to be water? I have oil."

"Negative on the oil."

Claire's pinky still blocked the hole in the fake light fixture. "What about blood?"

"I mean hypothetically yes, blood would work. But—"

Claire tuned her out. Blood it was. Keeping her pinky locked in the bulb, she slid a knife out of her forearm and pricked her right palm. A bead of blood welled up on her skin. It was like a high stakes juggling act, where one slip equaled total annihilation.

She took her time.

Astra had gone silent, apparently accepting the solution as the only possibility.

Claire withdrew her pinky and pressed her palm to the top of the bulb. The heat from the light stung her skin, but she ignored the discomfort.

Three, two, one, and her system blinked green.

Toxicity diffused.

"One down," she said, scanning the chandelier again. "Nine to go."

"Is there time for that?" Astra asked.

Claire reached for the next bulb. There'd have to be.

Andre seemed to be in no hurry. He'd been waiting for this, after all. Claire didn't get it. These people were just

Landry City citizens, living their lives. But Andre soaked in their attention, lingering on the moment like a soprano nailing a high note.

Claire gave silent thanks for theater people and their love of attention. *Milk it, Andre*, she thought, inserting her bloodied knife into the second bulb. *Milk it all the way.*

"I've been a model citizen," Andre said. "Exemplary, even."

"Thinks well of himself," Astra said.

Claire diffused a third bottle. A fourth. The skin on her palm was beginning to blister. She kept going.

Andre bent and slowly untied his shoelace. The audience watched in silence, and Claire wondered if they understood yet that this was no performance.

She diffused the fifth bottle. Halfway. She couldn't flex her hand. She ignored the pain.

Andre edged his shoe off, and his sock, revealing his metal foot. But that alone wasn't enough to shock the audience.

When he straightened, his pupils flashed red.

The crowd gasped.

Six, seven. Two more to go.

"I have made your opera house new, and yet you despise me because I'm half computer," Andre said. "I thank you for your endowments. You'll be handing them over more quickly than you'd originally anticipated."

At that, a handful of people rose out of their seats. Someone in the back tried for the doors. Based on the commotion that followed, they didn't succeed. It was all happening on the periphery of Claire's awareness, escalating panic she could do nothing to stop.

She diffused the ninth bottle, and her x-ray vision failed.

Andre held up a button, which, as a cyborg, he surely

didn't need. A detonator, rigged to shatter the bulbs under Claire's feet and release deadly fumes into the room.

She searched wildly for the last bottle. Without her x-ray vision, they all looked the same.

"Astra, how much trouble will one vial of that gas cause?" she asked.

"It'll kill you if you're right on top of it," Astra said, matter-of-fact. "In a room this size, everyone else might be OK."

People were running for the doors now, probably thinking bomb rather than gas. The guards at the doors held them back as more soldiers poured into the room.

Andre liked his drama.

"I can't find it," Claire said. "Guess I'm taking the quick route down."

Astra didn't respond. A quick glance confirmed that the battle had reached her, and she was fighting to get the doors open.

Claire fixed her hand on the chandelier. Before she could overthink it, she drew the laser gun out of her back pocket with silent thanks to Iz for knowing her shit. She aimed at the top of the fixture and squeezed the trigger.

Light screamed toward the chain, and the chandelier shuddered, glass cracking beneath her feet. Claire shot again.

The chain snapped.

The chandelier swept through the hall, with Claire clinging to the top. The room blurred around her, screams melting together as people dove out of the way, or tried to reach the doors, or fought the insect-like guards. Her monstrous ride bowled over a trio of masked soldiers before the chandelier landed between the seats with a crash that would have knocked anyone else to the floor. Glass cascaded away beneath her feet and she slipped, her weight tipping the whole thing forward.

Thank the stars for locking fingers.

To the right, Astra used the distraction to defeat another soldier. On to the next.

Too many. There were too many, even for Astra.

Henry fought, too, and Sam. Even Carlotta was hitting a merc over the head with a chair by the stage door.

Firmin hid in the orchestra pit, his tuxedo tails sticking out from beneath the piano bench. Claire didn't think he'd be much good in a fight, anyway.

She released her hold and leapt from the shattered chandelier, bulbs and chains clanking in her wake, and ran for the stage.

Andre waited for her.

"I'm afraid I still don't know why you fight me," he said. He had to raise his voice over the riotous clash of shouts and firing weapons. Smoke cut through the air, acidic. "Who are you?"

"You made me a cyborg," Claire said. "You killed my parents."

She dashed for the stage, stepped up on the edge of the orchestra pit, and leapt.

She landed, legs smarting, and tumbled forward in an awkward somersault. Andre was already on her, aiming a kick at her middle. Claire rolled away from his knife-sharp foot and jumped to her feet.

The room was absolute chaos, but someone had managed to get a door open. People streamed toward it.

It was all she had time to register before Andre was on her.

He'd gone without the mask tonight, because he hadn't expected any of the audience to leave this room alive. Did he trust his own soldiers that much, or had he planned to take them down with everyone else?

If she had to guess, she'd bet on holes in those gas masks.

Andre swung a fist at Claire, and she barely managed to evade it. She had to. His fists were made of metal. They'd put holes right through her.

"I don't know why you don't side with me," he said. "They can't treat you any better than they treat me. They don't deserve your protection."

Maybe not. But they didn't deserve to be murdered, either. Claire threw another punch and he caught it like he had in the vault, this time locking his fingers around her metal wrist.

"Transport A90D," she said, her teeth gritted with the effort of keeping him from pulling her toward him. "I was on it. My *parents* were on it."

Andre raised his eyebrows, surprised. He had the start of a bruise at the edge of one eye. "I didn't know anyone had escaped."

"I was just a kid."

He shrugged. "Far be it from me to interfere with a mission of revenge."

He wanted her to think they were the same. They weren't. Claire zapped his arm with a current of electricity, the way she'd done with Fay. It vibrated through his arm, seizing the mechanism, and he let go of her, stumbling back halfway across the stage. He whirled around, using the heavy momentum of his body to throw him forward again, and rushed her. He was fast, faster than she was, his robotic legs pushing him forward and slamming her into the side of the stage. A carved rose dug into her back.

"Say goodbye, little bird," Andre said.

He reached into his pocket for the jammer.

The shock on his face was beautiful.

Claire forced her hand into her own pocket, fumbling for the button on the side of the jammer. She pushed it.

Her computer system went dark, her limbs pressing against the wall as if to shove her through it. She'd been expecting the shift.

Andre hadn't. His grip slackened, his legs freezing him in place. Before he could recover, Claire punched him in the face.

She didn't need her metal hand to do that.

Andre crumpled, his legs dragging him down, and Claire shifted forward to allow the heavy weight of her body to fall forward and pin him to the stage. Not the most graceful way to defeat an enemy, maybe, but an effective one. Andre struggled, but it was too late. Claire maneuvered her right arm over his neck and allowed gravity to do the threatening. Andre stopped fighting.

If nothing else, he valued his life.

"Keyes," Andre choked. "He won't stop here."

The riot pulsed below the stage, doors opening, guards abandoning their stations. Claire's hearing was reduced to one ear, giving the scene a dampened, otherworldly feel. She thought about the glittering horror of the bridge explosion, the packed hover-rail station. Keyes was responsible for this, for all of this. The Green Cyborg was only a tool in his kit.

"I know," she said as footsteps pounded across the stage to her aid. "That's why I'm leaving."

26

CLAIRE

C arlotta pressed a damp cloth to Claire's palm and dabbed the blistered skin with medicine, clucking her tongue as she worked. "Nasty burn," she said. "Drink that water."

Claire obeyed, scanning the opera house as she drank. Henry leaned on the door frame as he talked to the police chief; he was the most capable of keeping the vinegar out of his tone, and therefore the most obvious person for that particular job. He'd get the AI hearts back into the city's possession, and maybe talk them into more traditional security measures. Or at least a guard or two. Astra was currently escorting an injured Sam home to rest, and hopefully stay out of trouble.

Claire didn't see Iz. She'd caught a glimpse of her after the battle, helping an older woman into a wheelchair. No doubt she was off doing similarly heroic things.

"So," Carlotta said, unwinding a swath of bandage from a roll she'd been keeping on her arm as a bracelet, "Angelique is our Phantom Angel. I should have realized. You hardly changed your name."

Claire had to smile, in spite of herself. "And you appear to be a nurse?"

Carlotta waved a hand delicately. "We all have surprises, darling. Me, I have seven younger siblings. Nurse extraordinaire." She paused. "Thank you. For helping Sam."

"I gotta be honest. I didn't really want to."

Carlotta snorted. "I've lived with the boy for six months. I can't say I blame you. But you did it anyway, and I'm grateful." She sighed and gestured for Claire to lift her hand for bandaging. "I suppose you'll be leaving Landry City."

"I thought you'd be glad. You'll be Firmin's star next year."

"Oh, no." Carlotta smiled. "The opera is without a manager, no? I think I'd prefer that role."

Claire nodded. She'd once dreamed of sloughing off her vigilante life to become Angelique D'Aae for good. It felt like someone else's life now. Compared with a chance to live as her true self, with Iz by her side—and Astra, and maybe more of her SATIS sisters—the old dream felt flimsy. Like a hope she'd fabricated to keep herself going. This was an adventure she'd never expected to crave.

Still, it would be nice to leave Landry City knowing someone was taking care of the opera.

Carlotta finished wrapping Claire's bandage, and rose, businesslike. She gave Claire a wink, and for a moment Claire had no idea why.

Then she saw Iz, hovering at the edge of the orchestra pit, hand on the half wall that separated the pit from the audience. Her hair was pulled back from her face, and she'd tossed a green usher's jacket over her t-shirt.

She was beautiful. She smiled, and Claire's stomach swooped.

Carlotta swept away, leaving them alone.

Iz stepped into the pit and came to sit beside Claire. For a few minutes they just looked out at the audience together, watching the bemused police officers as they pried terrified theater-goers out from under the seats.

"Thanks for your help with Andre," Claire said finally. "Sorry you had to get kidnapped to do it."

"I had the situation handled."

"Oh, of course, I could see that."

"The kiss helped."

Claire felt heat rush into her face. She hadn't forgotten the kiss—who could forget a kiss like that?—but it wasn't at all the one she'd pictured if she and Iz ever reunited. "Bit rushed," she said. "Wouldn't you say?"

"Definitely."

Claire wanted nothing more than to try that kiss again, to try their love again. But doubt lingered, stubborn. As if a portion of her heart was still jammed.

"You know what I am," she said softly. "Are you sure you want to...I don't know, get *involved* with me?"

Iz put a hand on her cheek. On the mask. "I'm already involved."

She tugged the mask away from Claire's face.

And Claire let her. There wasn't any use in hiding. Iz wanted her, and she'd take Claire for what she was.

Iz studied her face, ran gentle fingers over Claire's metal cheekbone, the steel hinge of her jaw. "Beautiful."

The second kiss helped, too.

THE POD FIT FOUR. Technically.

Comfortably? Well, that was another story. Claire was

never going to be comfortable on a spaceship. But Iz was here to hold her hand, and that made a difference.

The roof opened, the rockets fired, and Landry City turned miniature, the opera house transforming into a toy, then a distant ring, and then a smear of lights that ran into other smears of lights until Iz zipped the pod through a passage in the satellite belt.

From space, Landry didn't look like any other planet. It was a gemstone, the pride of the system. Her family had lived joyfully there. She'd fallen for Iz there. Her devotion to Landry City had been so entwined with her love of music that she couldn't have said where one piece of her stopped and the next began.

But Landry City didn't look like home anymore. Claire had a family again. With Iz's hand in hers, she turned to face the stars.

EPILOGUE

onor Keyes woke to the sound of his father's voice, and for a moment he thought he was about to die all over again.

He opened his eyes.

He was lying in a hospital bed, with *Traveler*'s disc-shaped logo stamped on the pale pink blankets, the smell of flowers and urine. Tubes jutted out of his hand. Bandages dotted his upper arms.

Everything hurt. Not in a vaguely sore kind of way, but with an insistent burning that radiated from the center of his body and threatened to make him pass out again. Conor squeezed his eyes shut, trying to remember what had happened.

Laura. She'd tried to kill him. Why had she tried to kill him?

Where was she?

When he opened his eyes, Dad's face filled the screen in the corner of the ceiling, his expression drawn with false concern. Dad wasn't here, thank the heavens; someone must have left the television on to keep Conor company. He recognized the columns of the Toccata System Council rising around his father, and could picture the panel of politicians listening intently as the system's leading expert in AI research manipulated them to his will.

Conor tried to pull himself up to sit.

His abdomen burned in protest. Tears of pain leaked from his eyes. He wiped them away, irritated, and settled for turning up the volume on the television.

"Just last week, the Star Leaders Academy lost control of their ship's artificial intelligence," his father was saying. "Now another AI has attacked Landry City. There is a gap in our understanding of how these computers function. Unless we take action, the tragedies will only increase in number."

The camera stayed locked on Dad's face as a woman's voice said, "I take it you have a solution."

Dread crept through Conor's chest and lodged in his throat. *No doubt,* he thought.

"I've been researching a patch for some time," Dad said. "Yes. I have a solution."

"It would need to be tested," a man said.

Dad picked up a glass of water from the table and sipped. The movement was slow and calculated, like everything he did. "Of course. If the council allows it, I would like to install the patch on Eding."

Conor turned the television off. He didn't need to hear the rest. He knew the Council would give his father permission to do whatever he wanted on Eding. They'd beg for his help, thank him for his generosity. Conor wondered if his father had been involved in whatever had happened in Landry City, then decided he already knew the answer to that, too.

He started to press the call button and thought better of

it. A well-meaning nurse might alert his father to a change in Conor's condition.

Wincing, he tugged the IV out of his hand and swung his legs over the side of the bed, retching as the wound in his abdomen sent tendrils of fire lacing through his body. There was nothing in his stomach to upend, but the contractions of his stomach made the pain even worse. He breathed into it, narrowly managing to keep himself from crying out.

Footsteps sounded down the hall, and Conor forced himself to his feet.

He was going to need a spaceship.

≈

End Book Two

≈

AUTHOR'S NOTE

Some of you sharp-eyed readers might be wondering whether the statues Claire encounters on the Palais grounds are references to classic literature. They are indeed!

The five women with the satellite-dish bonnets are the Bennet sisters from *Pride and Prejudice*; the girl peeking through the hedge is Mary from *The Secret Garden*; the old man surrounded by three figures is Scrooge from *A Christmas Carol*; and the wizard holding the sinister-looking ring is, of course, Gandalf in *The Lord of the Rings*.

ACKNOWLEDGMENTS

As always, it takes a village to publish a book, and I've got some incredible people to thank.

First of all, extra special thanks to my editor, Lynn O'Connacht. You made this book about a million times better than it was when I dumped it on your virtual door, in all its action-packed glory. You helped me turn it into something more. I'm so grateful for your savvy reading, your cheerleading, and your general awesomeness. Thanks so much for everything.

My writing group steadfasts: Chace Verity, Stephanie Eding, Leigh Landry, and Maria Z. Medina. You are my support system, so it only made sense to name planets after you. Chace, thanks so much for the gorgeous interior graphics—I love them.

Thank you to Sara Rauch, Jessie Kwak, Sara Seyfarth, and Killian Czuba, for your friendship and general creative-life supportiveness. Special thanks to Killian for designing my shiny Spells & Spaceships logos!

Thank you to the folks at SFWA for setting up a fabulous mentorship program. *Phantom Song* and *Parting*

Shadows would not have made their way into the world without your generous work, and I sincerely appreciate your dedication to helping new authors.

To all the book bloggers and bookstagrammers (whether we've corresponded or not), let me just say: THANK YOU. I'm not sure I've ever communicated with such a consistently thoughtful, kind, and enthusiastic bunch of people. You're such dedicated readers, and such kind supporters. You contribute so much goodness to the world through your love of reading, and for that, I'm so grateful. Y'all are superheroes.

Thanks to my family—Mom, Dad, Susan, and Shana—for always having my back.

Milo & Moshe—you guys give me the courage.

ABOUT THE AUTHOR

Kate Sheeran Swed loves hot chocolate, plastic dinosaurs, and airplane tickets. She has trekked along the Inca Trail to Macchu Picchu, hiked on the Mýrdalsjökull glacier in Iceland, and climbed the ruins of Masada to watch the sunrise over the Dead Sea. Kate currently lives in New York's capital region with her husband and son, and two cats who were named after movie dogs (Benji and Beethoven). She holds an MFA in Fiction from Pacific University.

You can find more of Kate's work, and pick up a free short story collection, at katesheeranswed.com.

 facebook.com/katesheeranswed

 twitter.com/katesheeranswed

instagram.com/katesheeranswed

ALSO BY KATE SHEERAN SWED

Toccata System Novellas

Parting Shadows

Phantom Song

Darkening Heaven

coming October 2019